Gimme Shelter Part Three

Kevin O'Neal

authorHOUSE®

AuthorHouse™
1663 Liberty Drive
Bloomington, IN 47403
www.authorhouse.com
Phone: 1-800-839-8640

First published by AuthorHouse 8/18/2010

ISBN: 978-1-4490-5375-8 (sc)

Printed in the United States of America
Bloomington, Indiana

This book is printed on acid-free paper.

Table of Contents

Introduction

Mary: (Hears a knock on the door.) Hello who is it?

Messenger: I have a telegram for Mary Bordowski.

Rev. Faust: (Mary calls St. Peters Cathedral.) This is St. Peters Rectory, can I help you?

Mary: (Crying and choking on her words.) It's Mary Bordowski, I need to come to the church to speak to someone and pray. Can you or someone else meet me there tonight?

Rev. Faust: Can you tell me what is wrong?

Mary: My husband has been shipped to the front lines in Vietnam. Can you meet me in the church in twenty minutes? I really need to speak to someone and pray.

Rev. Faust: I will be waiting for you inside the church. Don't go to the rectory; just enter the front doors of the church. (Mary enters the church with the four girls.) You look terrified. What can I do for you?

Mary: (Crying and choking on her words.) My husband has been shipped from the LBJ Power Plant to the front lines in Vietnam. Please pray for him and all of the troops. I want them home, I want them all sent home.

Rev. Faust: Lord hear our prayer. Look out for the souls and safety of our troops in their darkest hours as they do battle with the North Vietnamese Antichrist and bring them all home. In particular, watch over one Jack Bordowski, amen. Mary, is there any way I can see to your comfort? We have guest rooms if you don't feel up to driving or if you are too upset to sleep or take care of your children. We could have someone speak to you and your children.

Mary: I would like to stay for the evening. I don't know if I will be able to do anything until I know my husband is safe.

Rev. Faust: Come with me my child and we will see to the comfort of you and your children. (The scene ends to Gimme Shelter by the Rolling Stones.)

Scene One: A Trip to Hell.

Lt. Janzier: (At 03:00 early morning formation the troops of alpha unit are told they will be blowing up a military target by 08:00.) Gentlemen, this morning we will be patrolling a small town near Saigon and blowing up a school house which has become an enemy strong hold. We must watch out for ambush and booby traps while in the fields and woods. We have twenty minutes to put our war paint on and embark on our mission.

SPC. Jack Bordowski: (In a sharp tone.) Sir, the Cong have civilians as well as American Prisoners that have been tortured in that building. How do we get them out?

Lt. Janzier: (Yelling at Jack.) The enemy often moves prisoners out of targeted areas so they can negotiate with us or extract needed information. The government has ordered the building destroyed because of the loss of manpower trying to take the location. Who are you to question an order of the U.S Government or mine?

SPC. Jack Bordowski: I'm sorry sir; I will be ready to move in 10 minutes.

Lt. Janzier: We will minimize radio contact until the mission is accomplished or we have to call in artillery strikes. I need two good point men, Aikens and Bordowski, you're it. I will travel with squad one. We will be patrolling high brush and woods. I need my sharpest eyes and ears.

SPC. Bordowski: (While traveling through the high brush toward the woods both point men raise their right fist and stop. Suddenly they hear a machine gun cock.) Ambush, take cover. (As the machine gun and several M16 rifles fire, only the communications man is hit. He suffers a wound to the shoulder.)

Lt. Janzier: Throw smoke; don't fire until you locate the source of fire. (Lt. Janzier signals his M203's out. Aikens and Bordowski locate the enemy and open fire.)

SPC. Bordowski: (As he sites the enemy in.) This is from downtown Brooklyn; later mother fuckers. (Both hit their targets and send the enemy troops running for their lives.)

Lt. Janzier: (As the enemy runs.) Everybody open fire, kill them all. (As all enemy soldiers are killed off.) Great job men. We must push on; we have a 08:00 deadline to meet. I will call a chopper in to take the wounded man away.

SPC. Bordowski: (Not looking, Lt. Janzier walks past several men who hate him. Walking to a stick pit, SPC Bordowski tackles him to save The Lieutenants life.) Sir, look out.

Lt. Janzier: I don't know if I should knock your ass out or court martial you.

SPC. Bordowski: (Throws a rock caving the corner of the pit.) I'm sorry sir. I didn't mean to hurt you.

Lt. Janzier: Thank you Bordowski, some of these men must hate me. What makes you different? You stay motivated. You're the only man who wanted to see me make it home.

SPC. Bordowski: Sir, I took an oath. Part of which stated I would protect my fellow officers. I take promises to god and country seriously.

Lt. Janzier: Do you know what makes these men hate me?

SPC. Bordowski: Yes sir, you came back from Officers School nasty and showing us you don't care about us. Most of the men felt you bought us the way you did to look good for promotion.

Lt. Janzier: (As a helicopter picks up the wounded soldier, Lt. Janzier lines his men up and instructs them.) We must move on, charges are set to blow up a school at 08:00; all we have to do is hook a plunger to the wires and push it. The last intelligence showed women and children were moved from the building.

SPC. Bordowski: (As Alpha Company gets to the school, they quickly secure the area. SPC. Aikens sets the plunger to the wire and awaits a signal.) Sir, charges are set and the area is secure.

Lt. Janzier: Have the whole squad report back and blow the building up.

SPC. Bordowski: (Everybody takes cover. SPC Bordowski gives the signal and Aikens levels the school. While going through the rubble, the bodies of women and children are discovered. SPC. Bordowski starts screaming, cursing and crying.) Jesus fucking Christ, we killed women and children. I thought intelligence reported they were cleared.

Lt. Janzier: We had orders.

SPC. Bordowski: I should have disobeyed them.

Lt. Janzier: Settle down, the enemy lied and we must do what the Pentagon tells us.

SPC. Bordowski: I don't kill women and children.

Lt. Janzier: I see and smell body decay that would have nothing to do with what just happened. I will request a check be done to see if these people weren't already dead.

Lt. Janzier: (Back at camp.) SPC. Bordowski, may I have a word with you? What will you do when your time is up?

SPC. Bordowski: I will rejoin the police force where in five years I haven't killed anyone to date. It's a little nicer because I only kill if I have to.

Lt. Janzier: I will do what I can to promote you to Corporal. I would like to thank you for saving my life and would like to stay in contact.

SPC. Bordowski: What will you do when your hitch is up?

Lt. Janzier: I intend on leaving the Army and joining the Navy where I can build a new reputation. I will go back to taking the safest ways to do things as I did as a sargeant.

Major Brantley: (Five days later.) Lt. Janzier, I have good news and bad about our investigation. Your attack on the school was a smashing success. You didn't get a look at the large amount of weapons and supplies the enemy was storing here. We also found the bodies of sixty three Cong soldiers and civilians we have been looking for. All of them killed in fighting and couldn't be buried because of constant fighting. Unfortunately three people we were trying to recover were killed in the blast. All in all, your mission was weighed out to be a smashing success. The government also looked at the bodies of the women and children in the rubble. Only four were killed by the blast. It would be best for you to tell the men that no one was alive. At times, the enemy does things like this to us so we live with a guilty conscience the rest of our lives. Some Americans who are unstable will remain that way the rest of their lives. Get your men in formation and give them the good news only.

Lt. Janzier: Sir, what if someone should ask if anybody was killed by the blast?

Major Brantley: Simply reply that all bodies were already dead. News that we killed American Prisoners or innocent women or children could really send morale on a nose dive. News like this can also send some of these men mentally overboard. I will note this assignment as a smashing success in your fitness report.

Lt. Janzier: Sir, I'm not a hero for killing seven innocent people.

Major Brantley: You're correct there. But you and those men are heroes for destroying a large ammunition dump and enemy stronghold. You will congratulate your men and keep the rest quiet. A good officer learns what to hide from their men.

Lt. Janzier: At early morning formation, I will congratulate our men sir. I don't feel very good right now, request permission to leave sir.

Major Brantley: If you need time to lie down, go ahead. If you need sick bay or convalescent leave, don't hesitate to ask.

Lt. Janzier: (Sits in his cot crying and puts his pistol to his head. As Lt. Janzier puts his finger on the trigger, he reconsiders his decision and fires his pistol into the ground. This attracts the attention of the watch who immediately calls Major Brantley. Without so much as a fight, Lt. Janzier goes on convalescent leave and is flown to Germany where he is debriefed in a location in Ramstein, Germany. Lt. Janzier calls home with the bad news.) Hello dad, I'm calling you from Germany. I have resigned my commission. I can't tell you why right now, but my reasons were good. I will need you to pick me up at the Phila. Airport. I will call you back with the details of my flight.

Donald Janzier: (One week later at the Phila. Airport Donald Janzier sees his son looking so depressed.) Come here son, I can't remember you looking so depressed your entire life. Wait until we are in the car to tell me what happened. (The two embrace and get Tom's bags and begin their ride home.) What is eating you so bad? Were you treated badly by your unit or during the debriefing?

Lt. Janzier: No, I was declared a hero for killing seven innocent people and was asked to lie to my unit. I never knew everything wrapped up in being an officer. We are expected to use some degree of risk which completely goes against my thinking. One of my men was wounded because I took the fast and easy way there and we were ambushed. The men hated me so bad for it that they said nothing when I was walking toward a stick pit. I was lucky one man was on my side and tackled me before I walked on the stick pit and died. I can't believe my own men could want to see me dead.

Donald Janzier: More officers are killed by their own men than enemy fire. Many of them may have figured a different route could have been taken, or at least a safer one. Sometimes enlisted people think officers don't care about them. Many hate us because they have to protect us at the cost of their lives. Other enlisted people hate us because we are promoted on their work. We need to get you to a physiatrist to get you out of this.

Lt. Janzier: Do you think I'm crazy?

Donald Janzier: No, but I was informed by two sources that you attempted suicide and that you need all the love and support you can get. I asked your mother and sister to stay home so I could talk to you alone.

Lt. Janzier: Do they know?

Donald Janzier: Unfortunately they do. The letter was addressed to both of us. Major Brantley cares about you more than you think. I was involved in a worse incident than you in WWII. I was given coordinates to blow up a building up that was supposedly vacated by the enemy who was holding at least one hundred or more of our troop's as prisoners. Intelligence reported all troops and prisoners had vacated. After we blew the building up we went through the rubble, we found the American Prisoners had been left in the building. I needed a lot of help to get through and finish my career. It isn't easy to lie to your men, but at times you have to. This information stays between you and me. To this day I wanted no one to know. Whether you want to return to the military or not, you still need help to function normally. Let's get you home.

Lt. Janzier: (Gets hugs from his mother and sister.) Hi mom, hi Trudy. I hope your lives are going better than mine.

Toni Janzier: Welcome home son, why don't you settle in and relax a few days. If you need to talk, we are here for you.

Trudy: I feel sorry for you. Vietnam is not a place I would want to be. I know life was rough on you.

Donald Janzier: Tonight you need your family; tomorrow we will line up an appointment with the VA to begin the road to recovery. After that you need to decide what you want to do with your life.

Lt. Janzier: If things go right, I will reenter the service in the Navy. I can build a new reputation and not have to walk through bobby traps and ambushes. I only need to go through a forty five day course. I would like to make the Armed Forces my career.

Donald Janzier: (After several months of mental health he gets a letter from Major Brantley giving him a new title, Lt. Commander Brantley, and asking him to come to the Navy. The Lt. Commander was in contact with the Janzier Family the whole time. He informs Lt. Janzier he could get him orders to Hawaii and an extra rank for his specialty and experience.) Are you ready to return? Let's get you to the Naval Recruiter and see what turns up. I'm so proud of you I could bust.

Lt. Janzier: (After testing, Thomas Janzier goes Navy as a LTJG. and is ready to go to the airport. Saying goodbye to everyone, Tom hugs everybody and takes off for his forty five day course.) I can't thank all of you enough. I couldn't have done this without your love and support. I love all of you and will call.

Scene Two: A Warm Welcome Home.

Mary: (As Jack gets home and off the plane he is greeted by a wife with tears of happiness and four daughters.) Jack, over this way. (The two embrace and engage in a hot kiss.) Say hello to your girl's honey.

Jack: I've missed you so badly honey. (Jack hugs all of his girls.) How are my girls? I missed you so much. Let's go home and spend some time together. You're all getting so big. Honey, I'm finished in about a month. We have so much catching up to do. I don't think there is enough time. Let's find the car and head home. (Jack hugs his four girls and says.) Let's get daddy's bags and go home and do some catching up. Daddy has to get to know you and mommy again.

Mary: We'll start that tonight. I hope you don't leave us alone again. You aren't considering signing back up are you?

Jack: Not a chance. My last thirty days will be spent looking for a place to live and checking back into the police department. I also want to spend a good percentage of that time reacquainting with my family. I've missed all of you so bad. With some of the things I had to do, I don't want to remember I was in the Army.

Mary: If you need to speak to somebody, please let me know. I will be there for you. There are free psychiatric services for you when you are in and out of the Armed Forces. If you need help, I will be there for you every step of the way. We need to enjoy some of this time together knowing each other. But we have to get busy getting you started back on your job and finding another place to live.

Mary: I have a bottle of champagne to celebrate this evening. I already have dinner and will start a little after we get home.

Jack: Honey, don't go to any trouble. Let's go out.

Mary: Dinner has been in the stove for awhile and will be done in an hour.

Jack: What is dinner?

Mary: I prepared Lasagna. For desert the girls and I prepared a chocolate mousse.

Jack: You have a big evening in mind?

Mary: Between you getting to know your girls and me, it will be a big evening. (Whispers to Jack.) You wait until I have you all alone. That's when we have the real fun.

Jack: I can hardly wait. (Mary and Jack share a hot kiss before they get into the car.) I love you so much. (While riding home.) How are my four beautiful girls? You are getting so big and beautiful.

Dallas: (Battling with Danielle for a sippy cup of juice.) Give me that cup Danielle. Daddy, tell her to give me the juice.

Danielle: (Begins crying and fighting back.) Mommy, daddy Dallas spilled my juice.

Mary: (In a sharp tone.) Dallas, knock it off.

Jack: Dallas, if you stop crying, you can sit on my lap until you fall asleep. Please pick the cup up and give it to Danielle.

Mary: You are the only one who can win with her. It's been a rough year and a half. I bought some champagne to celebrate your homecoming. When the kids go to sleep we can settle in and talk. There is so much that you've missed. Some can be discussed with the kids, some we will discuss alone.

Jack: I swear we had two daughters. Darlene and Daisy, what makes the two of you so quiet. (Whispering to Mary.) Why can't they all be as quiet? (Dallas hears the comment and starts to cry.) Dallas, daddy was just kidding. Honey, please stop crying.

Mary: We will be home soon. It's time to welcome daddy home.

Dallas: I get to sit on daddy's lap until I go to sleep.

Jack: (As they get home.) Let's go inside now. I'll grab my bags from the car tomorrow. Let me get our two young ones out of their car seats. OK girls, let's go inside. (Mary gets the bottle of champagne for the happy couple and some soda for the four girls.)

Mary: Tonight will be great; this family is back together to stay. We'll show you everything you've missed and welcome you home. (Mary hands Jack a glass of champagne and the girls get soda.) I propose a toast to having your father home and being a family again. Let's drink up girls. Jack, let's go into the living room and sit down. I will give you the photo albums and show you everything you have missed. These are pictures of Darlene and Daisy's first steps. Unfortunately, you missed their first words too. These pictures are of Dallas and Danielle's fourth birthday. There are two familiar faces.

Jack: Did they stay in contact the whole time?

Mary: We were well supported from all sides. Your father was the person I saw the most. I almost couldn't keep him away. He really loves those four girls and me. He constantly took us out and kept our spirits up. Your father always told the girls and me that you can't kill an Irishman and that's what your father is. I really love your parents. Half the time I was busy making or repairing dresses and watching the girls he would call and take lunch with us. He couldn't stay away from his grand daughters and me. Your father always said you were the different one in the family. He said that aside from one instance in your life, you always knew how to treat a lady. He also said you were the only one of the three boys who knew how to treat a lady. You are the only Bordowski in the last five generations to bring this family girls. In your fathers mind, this is a special gift. I really think he made excuses just to hold his grand daughters and tell them stories. Some of the old country and some cop stories. The girls just love him, especially Dallas. Whenever she was giving me a hard time, all your father had to do was rock and hold her and she would drift off to sleep. He has the same effect on her as you do.

Jack: (Dallas is fast asleep like old times on daddy's lap.) You mean like right now. I missed being with all of you so badly it hurt. Let's get the kids to bed and get to know each other again. (Mary and Jack put the two girls to bed.)

Mary: (Mary pours another glass of champagne.) Why don't you make our next toast?

Jack: A Toast to returning to the girls I love most. I really missed you, my one true love. (The two intertwine arms, toast and begin a hot kiss. Jack leads Mary to the couch as the two of them put their drinks on the table and break into a hot French kiss. The two wrap their arms and legs around each other and begin touching and stroking one another.)

Mary: (Begins loosening her blouse and skirt, then she lies back slowly.) I love you Jack, make love to me. (As Jack quickly undresses Mary slows him down.) Let's take our time about this. It's our first time in a year and a half and we have all night. I really want to take our time and show you how much I love you.

Jack: I love you too. Let's have one more toast to us. We'll make it a loving cup. (The two sip their champagne and settle in wrapped around each other under a blanket.) I missed moments like this so bad it hurt.

Mary: (While kissing Jack, Mary places his hands on her breasts.) Let it hurt no longer. Touch me all over. Do everything slowly and light honey. (As Jack begins combing Mary's breast and nipples she begins breathing harder and she slips her tongue in Jacks mouth. Mary whispers in Jack's ear.) Touch me down low and feel how excited you get me. (Jack puts his first two fingers in Mary's well oiled tunnel of love and she begins to moan. Mary pulls her legs back and places his hardened flesh inside of her.) AHHH! AHHHH! Stroke it slow and deep Jack AHHHH! AHHHH! It feels so good Jack, it feels so good. Oh god, I'm cumming Jack. I'm cumming so hard. (Wrapping her arms and legs tightly around Jack, Mary orders him.) Push harder honey, push it harder.

Jack: (Mary pulls her legs as far back as they will go, then puts them around his neck.) Honey, you have me so excited. (As Jack explodes inside of Mary he lies on top of her. Both have racing hearts.) I love you so much Mary. I don't know what I would do without you. I will love you until death do us part.

Mary: I love you too. I want to lie here with you and hold each other. I missed your warmth from your body to your presence. Everything will be so much better with you home. We can talk about our future plans tomorrow, if your ready, we can take this to the bedroom.

Jack: That would be fine with me. You can still wear me out. (The two make love again and turn in curled up to each other. As the two wake up they talk about future plans.) Honey, if you don't mind I would like to visit Chief O'Hara. I want to let him know my first date of availability.

Mary: Make sure you spend your last four weeks or at least three of the last four weeks with your children and me. We also need to talk about where we will be living and where I will be working my business from. I have been able to save a few thousand dollars while you were away. As you can see, I have done well with my business. The Base Commanders Wife had me work on a ball gown for her and I did some quick repairs on his uniform to. I have a lot of business from the enlisted and officer communities. I have also been able to buy a lot of new furniture. (While Mary is cooking breakfast, Jack talks to her and the girls.) How are my four little girls? Jack puts his two little girls on his lap and Dallas starts up immediately.)

Dallas: Daddy, I want to sit on your lap. Put Daisy and Darlene down.

Mary: Dallas, wait your turn. Daddy rocked you to sleep last night; he hasn't even held Danielle yet. Stop being so greedy or I'll send you to your room.

Dallas: (Looks at her mother with a sneer and with some attitude answers.) All right mommy, but I claim daddy tonight and I want to sit on daddy's lap after breakfast.

Danielle: (Crying and reaching for daddy.) Daddy, I want to sit on your lap. I want daddy now.

Mary: Girls, daddy will hold you one at a time.

Danielle: I want to sit on daddy's lap in the living room.

Jack: Honey, when I'm finished feeding Daisy and Darlene, I will take Danielle when we go to the living room. I wonder how long this popularity will last. (After everybody has been fed, the family moves to the living room. As Jack sits on the rocking chair, Dallas quickly sits on his lap and Danielle starts to cry.) Now Dallas, you sit by mommy until I sit with Danielle. I haven't spent any time holding her.

Dallas: (As Danielle cries louder and reaches for Jack.) No daddy, I want you now.

Mary: Dallas, go to your room now. What you did to Danielle was rotten. I will call you when you can come out. Get in your room now. She always tries to push the other girls around and I can't stand it. I always have to put Dallas in her place.

Jack: Come to daddy Danielle. How is my quiet little girl? I haven't forgotten you. Honey, can I have a sippy cup for Danielle. What kind of juice do you want? (Danielle says orange juice.) Mary, can we have a sippy cup of orange juice? Thank you, a daddy-daughter talk isn't complete without something to drink.

Danielle: (Out of nowhere Danielle asks a tough question.) Daddy, did you ever shoot anyone with your gun?

Jack: (The question catches Jack off guard.) No honey, I was at a quiet beautiful area with no fighting.

Mary: That isn't what you should be asking your father. You should know he would never hurt anyone. I hope you will let me get a word or two in before you go.

Jack: I'm in no rush. What is on your mind?

Mary: In a few days, can we look for another place to live in the Brooklyn area? It should be half way between where we will be working. Col. Hartley said he would rent space retail space to me reasonably. I have enough to pay for a year and get us a down payment on a house or apartment. This leaves me within reach of the military community and gives me access to the private sector.

Jack: You always were a great planner. Let's start looking soon.

Mary: Honey, I'm sorry about what Danielle asked you.

Jack: I'll be all right, don't worry about me. Any issues I have can be discussed with a VA counselor for free. If it's all right with you, I want to visit the chief and tell him when I'm available.

Mary: That is fine with me. Be back for dinner.

Jack: I will be gone no longer than two hours. I don't want to be away from my five favorite girls for too long. (Jack tells the chief when he is available and lines up an appointment with the psychology dept. to discuss his problems.)

Mary: (Talks to Col. Hartley and gets the shop space for her business.) Jack, I called Col. Hartley and he will rent me some retail space for $200.00 per month as a favor for what I did on short notice for him and his wife. We can start house or apartment hunting at any time. (Three months after finding an apartment and both working hard, Mary comes home from the doctors with great news.) Honey, I've got great news, I'm pregnant.

Jack: Honey, that's wonderful. How far along are you?

Mary: I'm two months pregnant. Honey, when my lease is up I will still be pregnant. Can I bring my business home? I've never been able to breast feed and the expense of daycare is killing us. I will leave notice of where I can be reached for business and care for our girls all day. (With a loving look in Mary's eyes.) Honey, please let me take care of my family at home.

Jack: (With a loving look back and hot kiss to begin celebration.) Why not, move home when you are ready. We will save money and you'll be a lot happier.

Mary: I got a good wine to celebrate with. I love you honey.

Jack: Honey, isn't this how we got here?

Mary: Yes, but we got a break, I'm only carrying one child. Since I'm already pregnant, one baby can't turn into two.

Jack: (Laughing and hugging Mary.) All right, we will celebrate another Bordowski child. I love you too. (The two celebrate and laugh all night.)

Mary: (In her eighth month begins moving things home and when her year is up, Mary turns her keys in.) Jack, I'm so excited. I'm within a month of my due date. I hope it's a boy for you. What are you hoping for?

Jack: Just a healthy baby. The sex doesn't matter.

Mary: I still want you thinking of a boy's name.

Jack: What name do you want if it's a girl?

Mary: I have already given that thought. If you don't mind I will name her Deirdre.

Jack: Honey that is a beautiful name.

Mary: (Three weeks later while in the shower.) Oh Jack, my water broke. Can you see if the chief will let you off for the day?

Jack: (Calls Chief O'Hara to get some time off.) Hello chief, I'm in a bind. My wife had her water break in the shower. Can I get some time off?

Chief O'Hara: Well, congratulations are in order. I will have you out on leave. Make sure you come by in a day or two to fill out your leave papers. Don't worry, we'll cover you. Good luck, enjoy the company of your wife and new baby.

Jack: I owe you big time chief. I'll see you in a day or two.

Chief O'Hara: We'll see you then.

Jack: Great news honey, he gave me what I needed. I only have to stop in to the department within a few days. What are you doing honey? We have to get going now.

Mary: (As Jack begins to pace.) Please sit down and relax. I want to do my hair and nails. I also have to pack my bag. My contractions aren't bad.

Jack: (Still pacing around.) I would still feel better if we were on our way. We do have to drop the others off at mom and dad's house.

Mary: (In a slightly elevated voice.) Jack, I'm the one delivering this baby. I'll let you know when it's time to go. (On the way to the hospital, Mary looks at Jack and smiles.) I'm so excited. Not that it really matters, but it would be nice if this baby was a boy. I love you so much honey. We have to be quick at mom and dads, the contractions are getting harder.

Jack: (With Mary uncomfortable in the front seat. Pat and Melanie Bordowski come up to say hello to Mary who really isn't in the mood.) Hello mom and dad. Here we are again.

Pat: (Opens the van door.) Come to Grand-Pop my pretty little ladies. What are you hoping for?

Melanie: Pat, it doesn't look like she feels like talking right now. The two of you should be on your way.

Mary: Mom has a point. We'll call when the baby is born. Please let us go dad.

Pat: (Yelling as he closes the door.) I hope it's another girl.

Mary: (Speaking loud while contracting.) Jack, step on it or we'll find out what we are having here in the van.

Jack: Oh no we won't. (Jack flies off to the hospital and a beautiful little girl is born.) Honey, I love you so much. Odd thing, she doesn't look like any of the other kids or us.

Mary: You're right; she takes after your father with the hair and some of his features. Deirdre is so beautiful.

Jack: Yes, I now have six gorgeous women at home. I love you so much honey.

Mary: (The two share a kiss.) I love you too. Let me hold my daughter please. (The nurse wrapped Deirdre in a blanket and gives her to Mary who cuddles her.) Hello my little girl. Mommy loves you. (Deirdre cries in a low tone.) Jack, this is a blessing. She is so quiet and beautiful.

Jack: If that little squeak is what Deirdre calls a cry, I may get a full night of sleep. Do me a favor; don't let Dallas give Deirdre any lessons on being noisy or on getting your way.

Mary: You got that one; I'll no longer have a quiet baby. Deirdre may get that strong will Dallas has. I can only handle one.

Jack: (Things grow increasingly difficult economically and Jack can't cover all the bills even with Mary earning good money from the home.) Dad, I'm a little ashamed of myself. Can I borough three hundred dollars?

Pat: Yes, you seem uneasy. You can come to your mother and me anytime you need help. Is that all you need? A family of seven isn't easy to feed. I earned more than you think when I was a cop, watched over Sullies Yards and fought all those years.

Jack: (With his head down and almost in tears Jack buries his head in his father's chest.) I'm so ashamed dad. I haven't told my wife I can't pay my bills.

Melanie: Hard times hit us all. You can come to your father or I any time you need to. Please pick your head up; things are going to get better. We hear Chief O'Hara likes you. In the future that could mean great things. Don't think we think more of your brothers than you.

Jack: I feel like such a heel and like I have nothing. Both of my brothers are millionaires and I have to come to my parents for help.

Pat: Right now, those two can't hold a candle to you. I personally would like to kick both of them.

Melanie: Please Pat, please stop, I still love Michael and Daniel. Please say nothing. We don't have all the details.

Jack: Dad, are my two brothers in trouble?

Pat: That's what we don't know. They may have money, but the two of them can't hold a candle to you. I would like to kick the shit out of them. At least you're a good family man and that is where my definition of man begins.

Melanie: (In tears and pleading with Pat.) Pat, please stop, please knock it off.

Pat B: (Raising his voice.) All right, all right Melanie, I'll stop, but I'm not too fond of them. (Melanie storms off to the bedroom in tears.)

Jack: Dad, please take it easy on mom. What did they do to piss you and mom off?

Pat: I can't talk now, but will when I can. Right now I'm so angry I consider you my only son. Don't worry, mom and I will be alright. It's time you go to your family. Give your wife and kids a kiss from mom and me.

Jack: OK dad, call me if you or mom need me for any reason. Please do something to settle her down. Try to have a nice quiet night.

Mary: Well, what kept you? Oh that's right; you spoke to Chief O'Hara about overtime. Ask him about promoting to lieutenant. By the way, the girls know your schedule like clockwork, especially Dallas who was a pain. Dallas, guess whose home?

Jack: (As soon as Dallas sees Jack she jumps into his arms.) How is my little girl?

Dallas: Fine, what took you so long? You normally get home at four thirty; you're over an hour late.

Jack: I had to talk to my chief.

Mary: Dallas, be easy on your father, he told what he was doing this morning. What did the chief say when you asked for overtime?

Jack: I start tomorrow. I can work up to ten hours per day and sixth hours every week. Things should straighten up a bit more. It will be nice to have a bit more money.

Mary: Please only work some. I'll never see you and your girls won't know you. I didn't have this family to raise the kids on my own.

Jack: I will limit the time I work.

Mary: (With Deirdre now finished feeding and asleep.) I'm so happy; I always wanted to breast feed and be home with all of my children. Please don't leave us alone for a long period of time again. All of us are just getting to know you again. I wouldn't mind having a few more children with you before I start getting close to forty.

Jack: If we have any more kids, I'll have to go to the loony bin! With money tight that will even be on overtime, please ask me before getting pregnant.

Mary: (About a year a later Mary has a lobster dinner with wine for the adults.) During dinner, Mary pours wine and toasts Jack. To having a new child on the way.

Jack: (Smiles and thinks oh no.) That's great news. How far along are you?

Mary: About a month. This pregnancy is a lot different than the others. I don't feel the fatigue that I did with the others and I'm not getting as sick. I don't have all the depression I did. I felt almost the same with Deirdre, but I'm happier and I have more energy. Maybe this will be that boy I want for you.

Jack: I'll just take a healthy baby, but it would be nice if it was a boy.

Mary: I'm so excited; I really want ten kids or more.

Jack: (Jack keeps his thoughts to himself.) As long as we can make it work, I'll be fine with that.

Mary: Well girls, do you want a brother or sister?

Danielle: I want another sister.

Dallas: We have enough. I want a little brother to roughhouse with.

Daisy: I want a sister to play with.

Darlene: I want a girl.

Mary: I will cast a proxy vote for Deirdre. We want a boy.

Jack: I just want a healthy baby.

Mary: Come on Jack, tell us what you want.

Jack: All right, put me in for a boy.

Mary: Whether this baby is a boy or a girl. I'll let you name it.

Jack: If it's a boy, I'll name him Patrick after my father. If it's a girl, I'll name her Doreen after my grandmother. How does that sound?

Mary: Everything sounds fine to me. Those are nice names. Do you think we can celebrate tonight?

Jack: That is what got us here six times, of course we can.

Mary: (With a big smile and a loving look.) We will celebrate after the kids go to bed. I really want to spend some really close time with you. We can watch TV in the living room and curl up.

Jack: I love it when we curl up on the love seat or couch. Book me in for a date.

Mary: You're on; we will have a great night after the kids go to sleep. (After Mary puts the kids to sleep, she changes into a see through night gown and throws a robe over her to keep her warm. Jack sits down on the loveseat and waits for Mary.) Tonight's celebration is over a successful marriage and to our sixth child, may there be more. (The two lock arms and toast and share a kiss.) Time for the real show.

Jack: That liquor was really good. It turns a normally sweet kiss into a really sweet kiss. Where did you get it?

Mary: (They share a hot kiss.) I bought this when we celebrated the birth of our first two. (Mary loosens her gown and shows her see through gown underneath.) I really want you Jack. Make love to me. (The two begin kissing with probing tongues.) I love you Jack. Touch me all over. Take your time, we have all night. (Jack undoes Mary's see through gown and begins manipulating her breasts and sucking on Mary's nipples. Mary moans as she lays back in the loveseat.) Keep sucking on my nipples. It feels so good. Touch me down low. (As Jack massages Mary's clitoris she moans and begins to quiver.) Keep going Jack, keep going honey. I love you so much. Oh god I'm cumming, I'm cumming like crazy honey. (Mary holds Jack tight and starts pulling on his flesh.) Jack, it feels so good. I just love the way you make love to me. Let's go down on each other honey.

Jack: You haven't wanted that for a long time. (Mary gets on top of Jack and they begin oral sex on each other. Jack's flesh begins to really stiffen and Mary begins to quiver as she enters orgasm again.) Honey, I'm going to cum. If you don't want it in your mouth pull away.

Mary: Let it go honey, let it go. I'm so horny tonight. (Mary pulls her head away and sits on Jack's penis.) I want this to be one of the times you remember honey. (Mary begins a slow up and down motion with her hips.) Oh Jack, I'm starting to cum again. AHHHH! AHHHHH! You're so good to me honey. I love you so much honey. I'm cumming honey, I'm cumming. (As Jack explodes inside of Mary she lies flat against him. Still quivering, Mary holds tightly.) It's your turn to take the top.

Jack: (Mary pulls her legs back and tells Jack to make love to her.) I love making love to you. Hold me tight honey.

Mary: Put it in honey. Push it deep and slow honey. (As Mary inserts Jack inside of her, she moans loudly.) Oh god I'm already going crazy. Keep pushing honey; don't go hard honey, AHHHHH! AHHHHH! Keep pushing honey, keep going. Oh god I'm cumming so hard. Hold me tight and keep going. Oh god, oh god, oh god, start pushing hard honey, push it hard honey. (As Mary feels Jack begin to twitch inside of her, she wraps her arms and legs tightly around him. As Jack cums a second time, he lies on top of Mary and holds her.) I love you honey. I want more love tonight. (The two make love three more times that night.)

Jack: You are truly the love of my life. Somehow you know how to keep the magic of love going. It's time to bring this party up to bed. (The two settle in for the night.)

Scene Three: Death of a Great Father and Cop.

Mary: (Three months later calls Jack at work after she finds out Pat and Melanie are in the hospital after a car accident.) Honey, after the workday please go directly to the hospital. Your mother and father were in a bad accident. No one will give me much information aside from the fact they are alive.

Jack: I only have ten minutes left. I will be on my way immediately.

Mary: (Sobbing on the phone.) Please let me know how they are doing when you find out. My prayers are with them.

Jack: (Calls Mary in tears.) Honey, it's terrible. My father won't walk again and needs life support to breathe. He is out cold from the anesthesia. He will never want to live like this. When I asked the doctor about dad's future, he said it's too early to tell.

Mary: How is your mother?

Jack: She is badly shaken up and has a concussion. She has a broken arm which has a cast. She will be admitted for observation. I will be home soon as neither can talk now.

Mary: (Jack buries his face in Mary's chest when he gets home.) I'm so sorry honey. Do you need to talk? Are mom and dad at least comfortable?

Jack: Mom is in some pain. She has a broken arm and I didn't tell you about several broken and bruised ribs. Dad is still in the recovery room, the doctor doesn't know if he will live. I will ask mom what happened tomorrow. I hope dad makes it through the night. I was given the surgeon's number and hours he will be in the hospital. (The following morning Jack gets put on two days leave. Then he went to the hospital to speak to the doctor and see his parents. Jack visits Dr.Turner the surgeon first.) Doctor, what are my father's chances of recovery and getting back to life as he knew it?

Dr. Turner: He was lucky to live. I know he will need life support to live the rest of his life. I wasn't the only doctor to operate on your father. He had ten broken ribs, a broken leg and a broken arm. It was a bad car accident. Your father doesn't know it, but he isn't returning to life as he knew it. Your mother will be in a lot of pain and discomfort, but will fully recover in time.

Jack: Have you told my father the bad news yet?

Dr. Turner: No, he hasn't come to yet.

Jack: Thank you Dr. Turner. I'm going down to see my parents. Mom, how are you feeling? I hope you're not in a lot of pain. How did the accident happen?

Melanie: We were entering traffic from Murphy's Gas Station. A car came barreling in from 12th Street and hit us in the driver's side door. From what I remember, the brakes failed. The next thing I knew we were in an ambulance and on our way to the hospital.

Jack: Were the brakes the reason the car had to go to the shop?

Melanie: No, we got the car inspected.

Jack: Murphy left the car in his side lot with no light, didn't he?

Melanie: Yes, even your father wondered why the car wasn't in the front lot.

Jack: Do you know what place the car is being stored?

Melanie: I think it's still at Murphy's Station so the cops can investigate.

Jack: I'm going to pay Mr. Murphy a little visit.

Melanie: Jack, please don't handle this as a personal vendetta. Let the investigating officer handle this. Don't get yourself in trouble. I saw an officer last night and Chief O'Hara stopped in. He was comforting to me and upset about the condition your father was in.

Jack: Do you remember who is investigating officer is?

Melanie: Yes, it's Davie McGinty, an old friend.

Jack: Mom, has the doctor told you of dad's condition?

Melanie: (She begins to cry and Jack comforts her.) Yes, he said your father will need life support the remainder of his life. I don't think he will want to live that way.

Jack: Dad is starting to stir. Dad, how are you feeling? Do you know what happened? Do you feel it was an accident or a setup?

Pat: I was marked for death by Anthony Tucci. Those two brothers of yours showed me nine million dollars cash and look at that. Michael and Daniel both said they would be paid one million apiece for their work. When I asked who issued the bonds they bought up the name Anthony Tucci. I asked them if they knew who he was and they said yes and they also knew the bonds wouldn't pay but they didn't care. When I explained who he was and that they would be killed instead of paid, they wanted to make a deal and return everybody's money. Michael and Daniel returned the money and gave Tucci's whereabouts. In return they were allowed to keep their licenses and work on Wall Street. For their own protection I suggested they leave the area in the witness protection program. Of course I was refused. All this took was one phone call from jail to do with all the money he has. John Petrucci has handled contracts before and that is who hit us.

Jack: Petrucci was found dead two days ago. I can hardly wait to question Ted Murphy. I will bring him just short of death.

Melanie: Please Jack; let Dave handle this with the department. Don't get involved in something that's over your head.

Jack: All I want to do is kick the shit out of him until he talks. Murphy will give in.

Pat: If it wasn't for those two idiots that were given too much, now look at the shape I'm in. In my opinion, I have only one son.

Melanie: (Crying her eyes out.) Pat please, I know their lot of trouble, but why don't you love your other two sons. Please find the room in your heart you have always had. Why can't you forgive them?

Pat: Did you see everything I did for those two assholes and this is how we are repaid. I got the crap kicked out of me at least a thousand times with prize fighting and on the street. Now they have endangered our lives honey. For them it's anything for money.

Melanie: (Buries her face in Jack's chest.) Jack, I can't stand it when he gets like this. Please talk to him about forgiving your brothers.

Jack: I will mom. For now I have to go.

Melanie: Stay out of trouble Jack. For your information Pat, your sons were beaten up about a month ago.

Pat: (With a smug tone.) Wasn't that a pity? I have quite a lineup tonight; I see the two idiots and Dr. Turner. I need to see if I will be all right down the line. Get some rest and at least bring Mary with you tomorrow. (That night Pat sees Dr. Turner and gets the bad news that he will always need the life support just to breathe. Pat has the doctor list him as a no code.) Honey, please turn the machine off. You know I can't live like this.

Melanie: I can't Pat, not until everybody has seen you. (Pat lies to the two boys that he will be transported to a nursing home. Melanie will move in with Daniel who has the room. The next day Jack and Mary show up and Melanie is present.)

Pat: How are the two of you? Today I want to tell the two of you how proud of you and those five grandchildren of mine I am. Jack, when you were young we did everything together. Mary, a finer girl couldn't have married into this family, and of course you know how nuts I am about those five grandchildren I am. Jack you may not know that I knew of your field promotion and how it came about. I never let it out, but we have both saved and taken life. I really never wanted any of you to know. I killed about fifty Germans in an ambush. We still have the letter Second Lieutenant Janzier sent us thanking us for doing a fine job raising such a fine and responsible young man and how you saved his life. You don't know how proud your mother and I are of you. Here I lie at sixty-two years of age and I never told you how much I love you. (Melanie begins to cry and Mary holds her.)

Mary: What is wrong mom?

Melanie: (Whispering to Mary.) The man I've loved for years wants his son or me to kill him and hates his other two boys.

Mary: (Starts to cry to Melanie and the two hold each other.) Oh my God, I never knew.

Melanie: (Whispering to Mary.) It will have to be Jack. I can't kill the man I love. He asked me to do that last night.

Pat: We went through thick and thin together. From football to me teaching you good study habits and how to fight, to kicking your ass that one time which was our low point.

Jack: Dad, are you apologizing to me for knocking me out?

Pat: Like hell I will. I'm pointing out how close we are. The one thing that better come to an end is denying your Polish side. It was a Pollock who helped me with my school work, taught me common sense and how to fight and organize. If it doesn't stop I'll find a way to kick the shit out of you. The other two got rich but you're the only gentleman of the bunch. As I said, you're my only son.

Melanie: (Still crying on Mary's shoulder.) Michael and Daniel are your sons too. Why do you hate them?

Pat: Honey, I don't hate my other two sons, I just don't like them. Come to my bedside Jack, I have never so much as said the words, "I love you," or held you close.

Jack: (Crying and holding his father.) Dad, what is this coming to?

Pat: I want you to turn the machine off with the three of you holding me. Marines and cops die with honor on the job or with those they love and honor the most. I never knew what it was to hold any of you boys. Jack, you're so different from the last five generations. We weren't good enough to have little girls. You're the first that doesn't hit and you're a strong father that goes home all the time. Mary, I hope you don't mind my saying, I hope it's another girl. Jack, don't worry about the family traditions of having a prize fighter, cop, or soldier in the family. Traditions were meant to be broken. Jack, I have one final request. This family must be unified and it is your job to make every effort to start getting along with Dr. Carrington and get him into the family picture. Mary, I never hated your father and understand the ways of the world. I know a wealthy family would almost never want someone of the working class in. The only problem with that reasoning is that it didn't allow him to see the great young man that was marrying in. Please thank your mother for keeping the peace.

Jack: Don't you want to see all of us?

Pat: I have everybody I want here. Before you do this, your mother has all the instructions. Those other two aren't to have my ashes or see me again. It's time to turn the machine off. (All three hold Pat crying as he lets his final breath go.)

Mary: (Jack cries hard to Mary.) I'll be there for you honey. Take some time off and we will spend a lot of time together.

Jack: (Crying uncontrollably and holding his father.) I feel like I killed my best friend.

Melanie: (Both let go of Pat's body and hold Jack consoling him.) You didn't kill your father; you made sure that there was no more pain and started his way to heaven. When your father made his decision to die he said that in his case man intervened where he should not have. Your father considered death a blessing over the way he was going to have to live. I am a little upset with your father on his lack of forgiveness for Michael and Daniel. Please just agree with me when I tell them his heart gave out. I can't let my other sons know their father didn't want to see them.

Mary: I love him so much words can't describe it. Both of you were so good to me the whole time we have been married. Trust your mother and I when we tell you that you did him a favor. His soul is now in the hands of god. There will be no more pain, only peace in his new life.

Jack: Mom, I have to leave before Mike and Dan show up. I have to get some time off.

Melanie: Why don't you want to see your brothers?

Jack: Because I'd like to kill the two of them myself. All dads done for them and with all they have. The problem with my brothers is, nothing is enough.

Melanie: At least your father hid nothing from me.

Jack: That isn't all true mom. Do you remember when dad told you that Michael and Daniel were beaten up? He and I did that. They were beating on their wife and kids, drinking heavily and doing drugs, and having affairs. Dad went up to see Roxanne and the boys; she had a matching set and was crying. When dad saw her crying he pleaded with her to talk to him about it and where Daniel went. He called Sharon and she said the same things were happening and he went to the Bijou where both were having affairs. Dad called me immediately and we found both making it with girls in their cars. We let the girls go and kicked both of them around. To avoid a problem with you we all agreed on a story on how it happened. With the shape those two left their wives in, they're lucky we let them live. I wish I could say I'm sorry, but I see abuse every day and it makes me sick. I would like to kick them around over a few things. I will come back later when they're gone.

Melanie: Why wasn't I told of these things?

Jack: Because dad didn't want to upset you. I'm sorry I told you that, but now you know they aren't angels. It's up to you if you want to ask them, but you won't get the truth from them. (Jack is choked up on the phone to Chief O'Hara.) Chief, my father is dead, how much time do I have and can I stay out for awhile?

Chief O'Hara: You have three weeks of leave and four weeks of sick leave. Just tell me how much you want.

Jack: Two weeks should do.

Chief O'Hara: I have to tell you, your father was one of my closest friends and one hell of a cop. If you will, ask your mother if I can come to his service. A lot of cops including me would like to pay their respects.

Jack: I'll check into that. Thankyou for everything and we'll be in touch. (After cremation services Melanie takes the urn home and the goodbye party is scheduled two hours later on top of the apartment building where they live. Jack has a discussion with his brothers in private away from Melanie.) Dan and Mike, I would like a word with the two of you in private.

Daniel: Jack, we already started making our amens at home.

Michael: You don't have to get tough again.

Jack: This will not be violent. Just to the point. Let's talk in the dining room. (As they get there Jack gives them the news on dad's instructions in writing.) Dad doesn't want the two of you touching the urn to dump the ashes nor did he want either of you in possession of them. The only way it will be in either of your houses is if mom wants the urn. I understand that mom is moving in with you Danny. If either of you hurt mom, or your wife and kids, I'll personally kill the two of you. (Jack hands a copy of dad's written instructions to Michael and Daniel.)

Daniel: Dad must hate us.

Michael: I knew he had it in for us, but not this bad.

Jack: Dad didn't die hating you, he said he didn't like the two of you because of the poor examples the two wound up. I did this to avoid any fighting at the party. (The next hour was spent moving things to the top of the apartment building and future plans for mom. After the guests arrived Pat was eulogized by many. The guests ate and drank beer and whiskey.)Mom it's time to grant his wish to dump the ashes on his beat, do you want to do it or, both of us to do this, or just me.

Melanie: (Crying her eyes out.) I can't do it; you are his favorite son and should do this alone.

Jack: Mom, do you want the urn afterwards?

Melanie: Yes, I will take the urn and whatever ashes are recovered. It's great to see a lot of cops here. Are they on the street?

Jack: Yes, a few people are below.

Melanie: Let's start singing Farewell to Danny Boy.

Jack: (As everybody sings, Jack dumps the urn over the building, hugs mom, gives her the urn, and joins his wife.) I love you so much honey. I miss him so bad.

Mary: I miss him too. Your father was a great man. I'll never leave you until death do us part. One never knows, sometimes from death comes new life. If he comes back in any of our children we have, I hope the fighting I understand he did gets left out of them.

Jack: (After all the cleaning was done and plans to move Melanie to Daniels' House were finalized, everybody goes home.) I need to go home and relax for a week or so. (Jack and Mary embrace and go home.) I love you Mary. On my darkest days all I have to do is think of you and I can get through it all. (Later that week Jack sees a doctor and gets a vasectomy without Mary's knowledge.)

Scene Four: Making of a Great Husband, Father and Cop.

Mary: (Five months after Pat's death another beautiful Bordowski girl is born.) Honey, don't you want to try for a boy. When I heal we can start right away in a few months. Can I hold my daughter? Doreen is so beautiful; I just want to cuddle her. She looks so much like Deirdre; both came out with a head full of your fathers' dark hair.

Jack: Let's save talking about having another kid for when we get home. I want to enjoy the company of my wife and daughter. She is so beautiful and sweet. If we are lucky, she will have a pleasant way like Deirdre. They look and seem so much alike and she is such a quiet baby.

Mary: (Several days later Mary starts talking to Jack who is on two week's leave.) Jack, in about a month I will be all right to start trying again. Would you like to try for a boy? I would love to have your son.

Jack: Honey, I had a vasectomy done when I was home for dad's funeral. I have put you through enough.

Mary: (With tears in her eyes.) Why didn't you ask me before you did this? What will the church say?

Jack: The church doesn't have to know. It will be between God and us. Honey, I could barely pay the bills for five kids and now I have a sixth. I understand my vasectomy can be reversed. For now, I have to worry about feeding six kids. If things get better, I will reverse my operation. I'm so sorry honey; I just can't handle any more. (Jack carried Doreen every chance he got. By the age of two he rolled around on the floor teaching her how to wrestle and put socks on her hands and taught Doreen how to fight which mom wasn't happy about. Later she learned to play with a baseball and football. Mary let them do these things but didn't like the way Doreen was coming up tough.)

Mary: (As she sees Doreen roll on Jack and pin him.) Jack, did your daughter pin you again?

Jack: Yes, she really kicks my backside. Next thing you know, she will be knocking me out. I bought my little girl some gloves.

Mary: Jack, you've gone too far. Little girls play with other girls and dolls. She is growing up like a boy and will scare the opposite sex. She will never marry nor have children because men don't want a woman who can beat them up.

Jack: My daughter is my sidekick; she can do those things later.

Mary: Because of this kind of roughhouse play Doreen hits her sisters over nothing.

Jack: It's a phase that will pass.

Mary: I still feel you are raising Doreen to be the son you never had.

Jack: Honey, when she is older Doreen won't even look at these things and besides, none of the other girls identify with many of the things I like. Let us enjoy these younger years then she will be yours.

Scene Five: Loss of a Dear Friend

Dispatch: All units, watch for a tall white male approx. 6feet 4 inches heading into Central Park in a white El Dorado N.Y. plates 398 NDG.

Jack: (A tall white male gets out of the car and pulls an Use Machine Gun out. Jack quickly gets out of his car as the gunman opens up on his windshield. Jack quickly calls back for assistance. Officers Akers and Dickens answer the call for backup. Akers and Dickens, the suspect took off into the woods. He is armed with an Use Machine Gun and knows how to use it. Akers spread about fifty feet to my right, Dickens about fifty feet to my left. Take advantage of your cover, maintain radio silence, and get this guy.

Akers: (Makes first contact and takes a chest wound.) Ahhhhh!! I'm hit.

Dealer: (Sgt. Bordowski hides behind some rocks and trees. The drug dealer sees him and opens fire missing Jack.) Somebody is going to die and it isn't going to be me cop. Come out cop, I want to kill another cop. Come on cop, who will die, you or me?

Jack: (Jack throws a rock that the dealer fires at. Jack slips behind a rock formation and shoots the dealer in the head as he passes Jack.) Looks like you die, asshole. Go to hell, pal.

Dickens: Good job killing that asshole Jack. We have to radio for help. Akers took a bullet to the chest.

Jack: Sgt. Bordowski to dispatch, officer down, Sgt. Akers has been wounded in the chest and lost a lot of blood. He needs to be metavacked to the nearest hospital.

Dispatch: Copy Sgt. Bordowski, a metavack unit is on the way.

Akers: (Feels very cold and weak and as though he isn't going to make it.) Are either of you religious? Please say a prayer for me. I don't think I will see tomorrow.

Dickens: Join hands with both of us and we will say The Lords Prayer together. (Akers dies while the three pray before the unit arrives. Sgt. Bordowski is upset once again and starts loosing it for being a city cop.) The death of a drug dealer is alright, but I hate seeing such a fine cop and man die.

Jack: I hate using this weapon. I'm looking for easier duty.

Dickens: Where will you go and why? Where is it any better?

Jack: In the suburbs. I don't mind beating the shit out of a criminal, but I don't like killing them. I did enough killing in Nam. I'm not even for the death penalty.

Dickens: Where do your ideas come from? You don't think like most cops.

Jack: It goes back to Vietnam when we blew up a school building. There were women and children in the building and the government still ordered it destroyed. We were told that everybody in the building was already dead, I have questions on that. My Officer in Charge didn't give the announcement and was never seen again. Hopefully I get Lieutenant so I can get off the street and out of the area. (Jack is promoted to Lieutenant and begins applying for jobs from New York to Pa.)

Scene Six: The final Year Home

Mary: (Hears her husband come home at 2:00 AM. sees he is stressed, and knows he needs to talk.) Honey, I can see things haven't gone well this evening. If you need to talk I'm here for you.

Jack: This evening was terrible. I lost a great friend and had to kill a man. He was a vicious drug dealer who got what was coming. I hate killing and losing friends. I had to kill in Vietnam and that still bothers me. The other thing that bothers me is our lack of money. I hate borrowing money or just doing without because we don't have any money. I also need money to buy a house and all I can seem to do is borrow it. Unfortunately, I will have to stop being a city cop. I will apply for a position in the suburbs from New York through Penna. to stay close to home. (After church, Jack goes to Sullivan's Junk Yard to see if he still hosts prize fighting. Much to his surprise, Bobby Sullivan, Alias Sully, still hosts the fights.)

Sully: Jack, long time no see. I read about your father and I'm very sorry. What can I do for you?

Jack: I see you still pack fighters in as well as spectators from all over. How much does the unlimited weight class pay if you beat the champ?

Sully: The purse is $5000.00 if you beat the champ. If the loser lasts five minutes, they get $500.00. No one has wanted to fight our current champion in the last six weeks. I thought of offering him ten thousand dollars and telling him not to return as a fighter. He has never had to split a pot and no one has lasted a minute with this guy. I'm starting to lose fighting business due to this guy. His name is Jack McCluskey and is the three year running champ.

Jack: Don't pay him a dime; I'm going to kick his ass. Is the fighting still run by boxing rules? Do you still supply mouth guards? Do you still allow the two opponents to jape jaws at each other to get the adrenalin going? Does the challenger still get to choose if it will be fought out with gloves or bare knuckles?

Sully: All the rules are still the same. However; no fighting until all bets are taken. There is usually a crowd of over five hundred people and I have to take all bets first. You can't start talking to him until all bets are taken. Do you want knuckles or gloves; I have to let him know now. Get a mouth guard from Chuck. Does Chief O'Hara know you are here? He still oversees all action. I hope this doesn't get him angry because the only other cops who fought here were your father and Dave Mc Ginty. Wait here until I notify the champ he has a fight and I collect all bets. Hey McCluskey, today you have a fight. Point the idiot out. (Sully points to Jack. McCluskey yells at Jack.) Hey faggot, I'm going to kick your ass.

Jack: I'll knock your dick in the dirt, pussy.

Sully: (Takes all bets and explains the rules. Then he calls both fighters to center ring within four feet of each other.) Ok guys, no swinging until I clap my hands. (Sully claps his hands and the fight commences.)

Fight Scene

McCluskey: (McCluskey fires an upper cut that Jack side steps. Jack throws a heavy left to McCluskeys gut and a hard right to McCluskeys chin that drive him back and the fight is on.) Let's go faggot, didn't even feel it.

Jack: I'll make you feel it into next week. (Both get back into the middle and swing away. Jack takes a hard right to the eye and returns a hard left to the jaw. Both men begin swinging furiously and often. McCluskey connects on a right hook to the jaw while Jack fires a great combination that knocks the champ on his butt.) Let's go McCluskey. I'm going to kick your ass. (With McCluskey's eyes sinking into his head, Sully gives an automatic eight count and allows the two to continue to fight.)

McCluskey: You've been lucky so far but it won't hold up. (McCluskey hits Jack and knocks him off balance but he spins and fires a right hook that knocks McCluskey back to his butt. Jack backs off while another automatic eight count is issued and the two are OK'd to fight. As both fighters close in on each other, they begin swinging away. McCluskey knocks Jack on his ass with a good combination. After the count of six Jack is back up and the fight starts again. As both egg each other on. Jack lands two sets of high crosses knocking McCluskey to his ass again.)

Jack: Count him out Sully, this fight is over. (Jack goes home $5000.00 richer but has a matching set and a bloodstained shirt.) Hi honey, I've got great news, I won my fight. We are $5000.00 richer and now I can start paying some bills.

Mary: Jack, you look terrible, you have a pair of swollen shiners. For all I know you have a broken nose. Look at the poor example you set fist fighting and gambling.

Jack: I like to eat and if you're going to gamble, make sure it's on your own abilities.

Mary: This disgusting fighting has to stop.

Jack: Prize fighting will improve our ability to get out of here. I will go to Saturday Evening or Early Sunday Morning Mass.

Mary: I will not willingly allow this.

Jack: This is one fight you lose.

Doreen: (She is about three years old and her father is her hero.) Mommy, let daddy alone. (Jack and Doreen walk into the kitchen to get something to eat.) Daddy, I want to see you fight.

Jack: I will show you how I earn some great money. Come with me Sunday, and then you will see how daddy beats up bad guys.

Doreen: You are my hero daddy. Can you teach me how to fight?

Jack: Yes, you will see how on Sunday, but you can't say anything to mommy (Jack quickly sneaks out the door with Doreen and they go to The Yards.)

Doreen: Daddy, are you going to fight? Will you win?

Jack: How can I lose with my favorite little girl cheering me on? Before I fight we have to eat breakfast, then we will meet a friend of mine.

Doreen: What is his name daddy?

Jack: His name is Mr. Sullivan. He will be watching you while I am fighting. (Jack introduces Doreen to Mr. Sullivan.) Mr. Sullivan, meet my little pride and joy Doreen. Doreen, Mr. Sullivan will be watching you while daddy is fighting.

Doreen: Hi Mr. Sullivan I'm Doreen.

Sully: Hi Doreen, I'm Mr. Sullivan. I will be watching you a little while. Jack, she is so beautiful, I will watch her like a hawk. You have to get ready, your challenger awaits you. If you want to place a bet on yourself the return is only one to one. (Jack hands Sully one thousand dollars and both fighters are called to the center of the ring. Sully tells each no swinging until he claps. If a fighter goes down the other has to fall ten feet back. Jack's opponent's name is Tom Mackie and he is loud and obnoxious.)

Tom: Sully, back out and clap your hands so I can kick this guy's ass. (As soon as Sully backs out, the two opponents egg each other on.) Come on faggot, I came here to kick your ass and win some money.

Jack: Oh yeah, bring it on puss. I want to see what you have.

Fight Scene

(Doreen is at Sully's side cheering her father on. Sully claps his hands and Tom smashes Jack in the eye. Jack responds by breaking Tom's nose with a hard left jab. Jack quickly ducks a right and blocks a left. Holding Toms left arm, Jack quickly smashes a combination home hitting the left eye and right cheek. Tom returns two hard punches to the stomach and an upper cut that knocks Jack on his ass. Sully gives Jack an eight count and signals the two into action. Tom gives Jack a left to the mouth drawing some blood. Jack returns a sharp combination cutting Tom's cheek and lips. This backs Tom out.)

Jack: My blood is as red as yours, asshole; get in here and let's finish this.

Tom: Bring everything you have. You're going down today.

(Jack ducks a hard right and gives Tom a hard upper cut that knocks him on his ass. As Jack backs off, Sully moves in with the ten count and Jack retains his title.)

Sully: Beautiful job, you're a great fighter and your little girl was so good. Doreen cheered you on all the way.

Doreen: You're the best daddy. Let me kiss your booboos and make them feel better.

Jack: Thank you honey, Sully I need to pick up the pool money and pot. I earned six thousand dollars today. Thank you for watching my daughter. Can I bring her back?

Sully: Yes, she was so good.

Doreen: Is this how you earn your money daddy?

Jack: This is called side money, it helps us pay bills and eat.

Mary: (At the end of the fight Jack has an array of cuts and bruises to be tended to. Jack needs to be stitched up on his inner upper lip and comes home to a blasting from Mary.) Jack, I want a word or two with you now about fighting and having the nerve to bring your little girl around a bunch of drunks and gambling bums. You're lucky I don't add to your assortment of cuts and bruises. Next time I catch her going to a rumble you will sleep with the dog.

Doreen: Let daddy alone, I had lots of fun. A nice man named Sully watched me while daddy fought.

Mary: (Sharp nasty tone.) Jack, you let that bum, Sullivan, watch our daughter. Tonight you sleep on the couch. Doreen, did he smoke a big cigar, drink a beer and curse a lot.

Doreen: Yes mommy, he smokes and drinks, but Sully only cursed when daddy hit the ground.

Mary: How many times did daddy hit the ground?

Doreen: Only one time mommy. Daddy really kicked the other guy's butt.

Mary: Honey, you have to stop your father from fighting. He needs stitches in his upper lip.

Doreen: Daddy, will you be all right?

Jack: Yes honey, I will be just fine.

Mary: Jack, have you learned your lesson yet?

Jack: Yes, prize fighting is very profitable.

Mary: (After Jack gets stitched up, Mary greets Jack home with tears in her eyes with all six girls.) Jack, I have to level with you. I not only don't like you bringing Doreen around a bunch of drinking, smoking and cursing pigs, I don't like you fighting at all. I hate seeing you go to the hospital and getting sewn up. Besides, I thought you stopped fighting in college. You know I don't like seeing you get hurt.

Jack: Honey, some things we can talk about and some things we can't. You wanted me off the street and I transfer to narcotics soon. I won't like being a surveillance man or heading that department, but I'll get through it. As far as prize fighting, I'll protect my title until I lose it. With six kids we don't have the money to leave the area or get a house in the city.

Mary: If you bring your daughter there again, we will settle the matter out back and you will sleep with the dog. Remember, we have a good Catholic Household and we are supposed to set a good example. Prize fighting makes us look like animals.

Jack: Honey, no matter how you look at it, you want to leave New York so I can have easier duty and we have no money saved to get an apartment or house. The second point I need to bring up is that pray all we want, the Lord only helps those who helps themselves. All the money you and I earn does is pay our expenses. Sometimes we aren't that lucky. The fighting money goes into the bank for a new house and better way of life.

Scene Seven: The Penalty Phase.

Mary: (One month later.) Jack, your mother called very unhappy and crying. She said Michael was found shot to death at The Lions Mark Hotel. Daniel turned himself in to the police and admitted to fraud. She is living at Daniels house and I don't think she likes it.

Jack: The thing she doesn't like is that dad was right. I just know those two were up to something. They must have embezzled money from some powerful people. I will visit Daniel today. (Jack gets permission to see his brother and has a conference that day.) Daniel, you didn't have to make dad's worst nightmare come true. What kind of shit were the two of you wrapped up in?

Daniel: We made our own fraudulent bonds and took Angelo Brazini for two point five million dollars.

Jack: You stupid fuck; Brazini is one of the biggest mob figures in town. He will try to get to you from the inside. Did you think you could hide from him? I can't really help you.

Daniel: Can't you bail me out?

Jack: I can't but I'll call mom.

Daniel: Mom spent all of her money paying our mansions off when she found out what happened and she is broken up about Michael's death. We lost a lot of money on the market and were in financial trouble.

Jack: (Yells at Daniel.) The two of you fucks never were any good. Sit here and rot. (Later that night Daniel hanged himself in shame.)

Melanie: (Calls Jack to inform him of Daniels death.) Jack I don't know how I'm going to live. Two of my children are dead within twenty-four hours.

Jack: I'm sorry to hear that. What happened to Daniel?

Melanie: Shortly after you left, Daniel hung himself.

Mary: (Three months later.) Jack, I got a call from Sharon. She said mom is dead. Sharon said she tried to wake your mother up and she was cold. Sharon called for a unit but they couldn't save her. Authorities want you to identify her. Sharon said she is selling the house and leaving the area.

Jack: Over my dead body. She stays until this mess is sorted out. (Later it is found Sharon poisoned Melanie and is convicted of murder. The kids go to Roxanne who eventually moves and rarely keeps contact. Jack is more determined to get off the street and more so out of New York.)

Scene Eight: Drug Bust on Forty-Second Street.

Lt. Harrington: (Lt. Harrington who currently heads the narcotics unit briefs Jack on a major drug operation at the Full Moon Saloon on Forty-Second Street.) You and the surveillance team will be drinking and observing those who buy and sell. You will have microphones hooked up to you and you will give description of buyers first. Then you will call in the backup team after a few buyers have been taken in. The backup team will make the bust on the sellers.

Jack: What is the name of the establishment we are going to?

Lt. Harrington: You will go to the Full Moon Saloon. A new gang has moved in and we need to get them out. By the way, Bordowski, my promotion depends on getting this done right so you can head this unit. If trouble breaks out you're to stay out of it. You're not to get too fucked up at the bar because we need you to point out buyers and sellers. The backup team handles all busts and problems.

Jack: Does this mean that if a fight breaks out that I can't get into it?

Lt Harrington: (Loud and obnoxious.) That's right Bordowski, I know you and your instincts, and you will have to stay still. The backup team is the only group paid to rock and roll. If I hear you got into a fight I'll suspend you so fast and long your head will spin.

Jack: (Jack gives a short disgusted answer.) Fine, fill me in on all details.

Lt. Harrington: You'll take the subway to Forty-Second Street South with the surveillance team; the backup team will already be in place. After identifying some buyers, you will make a drug deal with a guy named Darin Black. He belongs to a gang known as the Sting Rays. The reason we are chasing them is that they have killed people and we need to take them down. Most of the gang members are there from opening to closing. You will be wired so we can follow the transactions and you can describe some of the buyers. After we bust some of the buyers, we will take the gang down.

Jack: When do we leave to commence operations?

Lt. Harrington: After you are wired for sound you will leave at eighteen hundred with the surveillance team. For an hour or two you will identify buyers leaving the establishment. By twenty one hundred we should have enough busts to let you make a deal with Black and take the gang down. Because you work closely with him you will be accompanied by Officer Dickens. Both of you will dress in jeans and ratty clothing to fit in. Simply talk to the speakers in your shirt. We hope everything goes smoothly and take down happens by twenty one hundred. By the way, call your wife, she says it's important. So please make sure you call home ASAP.

Jack: (Jack calls home immediately.) Hello honey, what is it?

Mary: Honey, Middletown Police called and want you to return their call. You have to speak to Chief Harris. I think they want to make you an offer. Please call me back after you talk to him. I can hardly wait to get out of here.

Jack: If the offer is close to what I make or more we will be on our way.

Mary: I love you honey, best of luck.

Jack: I love you and will see you tonight. (Jack calls Chief Harris.) Hello Chief Harris, it's Lt. Jack Bordowski.

Chief Harris: Good to hear from you Lieutenant. Your record is quite impressive and we would like to have you aboard. How long would it take you to get here?

Jack: I would have to turn in a two week notice. By the way, what is the salary?

Chief Harris: It is forty-seven thousand per year.

Jack: That's more than I make as a Lieutenant in the city. I will be happy to come aboard.

Chief Harris: Report to my office at 0700 hrs in June 28th and we will go through orientation.

Jack: (Calls home with great news.) Honey, I've got great news, I got a seven thousand dollar raise in a lower cost area. You will have your wish and we're out of here in two weeks.

Mary: Does this mean you will stop fighting?

Jack: I will continue until we are in position to buy a house. Then I will throw a fight.

Mary: I can't wait until you stop fighting and we move from New York. I love you honey.

Jack: I love you too. I'll get busy writing my two week resignation. I still have a bust to do tonight. Don't worry honey; all I'm doing is surveillance.

Mary: Please be careful, we are so close to getting out of here. When you get home, I would like to celebrate, just the two of us. I will get champagne and turn the lights down low. With what you had done, we don't have to worry. Just promise you will stay out of trouble.

Jack: I will come home safely and enjoy our evening. (After being wired for sound, Jack and Officer Dickens are riding the subway to South Forty-Second Street. The music in the scene is Can't You Hear Me Knocking.) Ernie, I'm wired from head to toe. I'm going to enjoy the sights of Forty-Second Street and bust Dennis Black.

Ernie: Remember, don't start any shit. All we will be doing is observing and calling backup team for busts on buyers, and then we will do the deal with Black.

Jack: I will be writing my resignation while we are drinking and reporting the buyers. I can't believe I'm getting a seven thousand dollar raise and lower cost of living.

Ernie: Way to go Jack. Will it be that much better, you will still be a cop and our job is still dangerous.

Jack: I will not be a city cop any more. Some time will be in the office and some on the street. The big difference is that I will be in a nice neighborhood.

Ernie: How long have you been looking?

Jack: About a year. No suburban cop positions were open, so I put my resume out through New Jersey and Pa. My wife and I didn't want my insurance check raising our children. Hey Ernie, look at the hookers. Yo honey, if you have the time I have the money.

Ernie: (Fearing a pimp would be near.) Jack, don't start any shit with these girls.

Jack: I'm enjoying my final night on NYPD because when I bust Black, I'm going to break his face. When Harrington hands me a two week suspension, I will turn in my two week notice and tell him he still has narcotics. It's to all units, wire in for radio check. Twelve units within a two block radius radio in. We are about one hundred feet from the bar; keep your ears and eyes open.

Ernie: This place is a real shithouse; I can't believe there are beautiful women here.

Jack: Trust me; you will spend a lot of money to get one of these women into bed. Let's get some drinks and sit at the bar. Ernie, will you do me a favor; watch the customers while I write my notice?

Ernie: Sure thing Jack. How long will you be and what would you like to drink?

Jack: Five or ten minutes, please get me a seven and seven and a rolling rock. If you would, call the backup team with the three suspects leaving the pool room. That's where the scoring is going on. (Ernie calls the backup team and the cops get their first three busts. After writing his resignation, Jack enjoys drinking and calling in to the backup team who made fifteen busts and it's time to bust Black.) I can't believe he is openly dealing to everybody.

Ernie: He has used fear factor against rivaling gangs and the owner. Let's take care of this guy.

Jack: I will radio the backup team, but before they get here, I want to break Black's face.

Dennis: Hey guys, I have red and yellow cap crack. Which one do you want and how much?

Jack: What about two grams of red cap to feel nice?

Dennis: That will cost you two thousand dollars.

Jack: (Makes the deal.) Here is the money.

Dennis: Here is the merchandise.

Jack: Do you know if any cops are around? NYPD, asshole, you can come peacefully or I can kick your ass.

Dennis: Fuck you, cop. (Dennis throws a punch at Jack that is blocked and Jack counters with a right and left cross and an upper cut that knocks Black over a table.)

Ernie: Get in here backup, Jack is going to kill Dennis Black. Jack what are you doing?

Jack: I'm picking a fucking fight. We have to beat their asses. There are at least twenty thugs. (A big fight breaks out that the cops win. Black and the gang were read their rights and jailed. Jack took a punch to the mouth but it wasn't bad.) Ernie, I have to clean the blood. My wife and I will be celebrating leaving NYC tonight. I have to go home looking good for a soft light romantic affair.

Ernie: Good luck Jack, the department and I will miss you. When did you say your final day was?

Jack: My final day will be June 27 but I get the feeling that tomorrow will be the last day you see me. You know Harrington will suspend me for busting Black up and that will be it for me.

Ernie: You should go home to your beautiful wife and enjoy the evening.

Jack: I will see you tomorrow. (Mary purchases a bottle of champagne after the great news, puts on Jack's favorite perfume, a see through night gown and puts the kids to bed. Dallas, Daisy and Darlene all watch through a partially open door as mom turns the lights out leaving the room candle lit and greets Jack at the front door with two glasses of champagne and a hot kiss.)

Mary: Welcome home honey. Let's get comfortable in the living room. We're celebrating two weeks left in New York.

Jack: We celebrate about every night. You are so beautiful, especially when you wear a see through night gown like the one you're in.

Darlene: Do you think they will make love?

Danielle: Yes, when don't they make love?

Dallas: Do you think we will have another brother or sister?

Danielle: With what dad had done they won't have any more kids. It's time to go to bed.

Daisy: With mom's loud moaning we'll never get to sleep. Let me see, Dallas.

Dallas: Get away, I won't be able to see.

Darlene: Why don't both of you get out of the way so I can see or make enough room so all of us can see, the way mom moans, we'll never get to sleep.

Danielle: Can anybody see anything aside from shadows of two people in love?

Dallas: Just the shadows of two people kissing.

Danielle: Why don't the three of you come to bed and shut up. (The three quietly tell Danielle to shut up and go to bed. Dallas leans against the door too hard and all three girls quickly go to bed.)Try to sleep through mom's moaning and go to sleep. Even though it won't be easy, Deirdre and Doreen are already there. (The girls finally go to sleep.)

Jack: You are so beautiful honey, I hoped we would make love but I didn't expect this.

Mary: This toast is to a better life in two weeks. (The two toast and wrap their arms around each other and engage in a hot French kiss. Mary undoes the belt on her gown and puts Jacks hands on her breasts.) Touch me all over and make love to me Jack. I love you so much, words can't speak it.

Jack: (As he comes up for air.) Honey, you're all I see and want. (After awhile of kissing and gently sucking on Mary's breasts.) Lie back and spread your legs before I make love to you. I want to touch you and go down for awhile. I love you honey. (Jack puts his fingers between Mary's legs, and then he begins softly licking Mary's clitoris. She begins loudly moaning in ecstasy. Mary shoves his head between her legs.)

Mary: Jack, it feels so good. I'm already cumming. Oh god oh my god I'm cumming so hard. Keep going, keep going. It's so good don't stop, don't stop. AHHHH AHHHH! Get on top and make love to me.

Dallas: (Tiptoes back to the door.) I have to see this. What makes mom so loud and I wonder if it hurts. Does mommy see God when they touch? Damn it, they need to turn the lights on. All I see is mommy's feet in the air and I think she sees God when daddy is on top of her. Do you think mommy sees heaven? If daddy wasn't on top of mommy, do you think she would go to heaven?

Danielle: No, but the way she says oh god she feels like she is visiting heaven. I think mommy sounds terrible when she moans.

Dallas: I think it sounds pretty good and like she is enjoying herself. When I get older, I want to try it.

Danielle: Oh shut up and go to bed. At this rate I'll never get to sleep.

Mary: (As Jack came up for air, Mary wraps her legs around him tightly.) Put it in honey. (Mary moans loudly as Jack inserts his throbbing penis.) AHHHH! AHHHH! Push it slow and deep honey, slow and deep. Oh, it feels so good honey, it feels so good. (After gently stroking Mary for about twenty minutes Mary pulls her legs back as far as they will go.) Harder honey, push it hard and deep. Oh God, oh God, oh God, I'm cumming again and again. Hold me real tight honey, hold me really tight.

Jack: (His throbbing penis begins to twitch and he explodes inside of Mary.) I love you so much honey. Making love to you is so good.

Mary: (After holding each other and kissing on the couch they sit up and talk for awhile.) I want to propose a toast to the finest man I've ever known. Tomorrow I will begin looking on the internet at school districts. Anything would be better than this. I want an area with a good school district.

Jack: This move is for you honey, so make the most of it. Start looking at the housing market too. Let's sit back and enjoy each other's company and the champagne.

Mary: How did the sting go?

Jack: Fine honey, we cleaned a gang out of the Full Moon Saloon.

Mary: Did you stay out of trouble?

Jack: I busted the ring leader up and we busted the gang. Not bad for a night's work.

Mary: Will you get in trouble for fighting?

Jack: We'll find out tomorrow.

Mary: I'm so happy that I don't care right now. (The two make love several more times and turn in. The next morning Mary gabs with Jack before work.) Have you turned in your two week notice?

Jack: That is ready to turn in this morning. I hope they will let me work the final two weeks.

Mary: Will news of your beating on Dennis Black get back to Lt. Harrington?

Jack: Yes, he will see the damage when he questions Black.

Mary: Do you feel you will be suspended?

Jack: Yes, this will probably be my final day of work for NYPD. Don't be surprised to see me home early. If I'm home early, we can all go out to eat. If I'm suspended, we can head to Bucks County and start house hunting.

Mary: Tomorrow are you going to fight or go to church early?

Jack: I'm going to fight early. I will try to score a swift victory and take as little punishment as possible. I will have two things for Lt. Harrington, who I never got along with, a challenge in the ring and my two week notice which should slow his promotion up and piss him off.

Mary: Hopefully you're not suspended. Try to stay cool headed until you finish. I can't wait until you stop fighting.

Jack: (Heading out the door.) That stops when we buy a house in Pa. I have to get to work honey.

Mary: (Gives Jack a hot soft kiss.) Let me know what is happening. I will be home looking up school districts.

Lt. Harrington: What the fuck did you do?

Jack: (With a big smile.) What did I do to whom?

Lt. Harrington: Why was Black so busted up asshole?

Jack: He swung at me when I showed my badge. At least we got the bust.

Lt. Harrington: It wasn't to bust him, you were to make a deal, call in the backup team and let them take him down. Black is in the hospital and he should be in a cell. I have your two week suspension written.

Jack: I have a present that will put your promotion on hold more than two weeks; it's called my two week resignation so fuck you, asshole.

Lt. Harrington: I ought to knock your ass out.

Jack: (Loud and nasty.) If we weren't at work I would take you up.

Lt. Harrington: Take a shot at me now if you think you can get away with it.

Jack: I wouldn't like to be fired. Why don't you take me on at the yards? The prize is $5000.00 if you take me out. If you last five minutes and lose you get five hundred dollars.

Lt. Harrington: I'm a gentleman unlike you.

Jack: Take me on in the spar ring; everybody would love to see that.

Lt. Harrington: Being suspended means you are to be off the property.

Jack: (Smiling as he walks out.) Thought so, you not only don't have what it takes, and you never will. Later puss, I'm going home to enjoy my new life and start house hunting.

Mary: (Jack comes home smiling.) Did Lt. Harrington suspend you?

Jack: Yes, so we have two weeks to go house hunting. Which brings to mind, did you find an area you want to look at?

Mary: Yes, I want to look at some houses in Upper Orchard or Snowball Gate, they are in Middletown.

Jack: We will go house hunting together for the next couple of weeks. (The Bordowskis rent two rooms at the Sheraton and started house hunting. Mary fell in love with a house at 122 Upper Orchard Drive and their offer was accepted. Mr. Thomas Murdock watched the deal closely. Mr. Murdock looked up the Bordowski Family up on the internet and didn't like what he found. Lt. Jack Bordowski was the new Lieutenant replacing Lieutenant Gold who was fired for corruption. He was on Murdock's payroll and for some time, justice was for sale. Mr. Murdock decides to stop in settlement to make the Bordowskis an offer not to buy the house.

Scene Nine: A Tough Time Settling.

Mr. Dailey: (Everyone is at the settlement table, Mr. Dailey the banker, Mr. Murdock and the Bordowskis.) Mr. and Mrs. Bordowski, Mr. Murdock would like to make you an offer, Mr. Murdock, please proceed.

Mr. Murdock: Mr. and Mrs. Bordowski, I would like to offer you this check for $85,000.00 not to settle on the house you are bidding on.

Jack: (He looks at Mary and she says no.) Why don't you want us here sir.

Mr. Murdock: Your family doesn't fit the neighborhood.

Mary: (With a choking in her voice.) What could you mean by that?

Jack: Keep your money Murdock.

Mary: That house is ours.

Jack: (With bad aggravation.) So you don't feel my family is good enough to live around you. There is more class in my little pinky than ten of you, you plastic son of a bitch.

Mary: (With lots of aggravation.) You have a heck of a nerve speaking to us like this. When we move in we will not wish to know you or your family.

Mr. Murdock: I will sweeten the pot. I will offer you an extra $100,000.00 to resign and move back to New York. I know how you got the money for the large down payment you have and you are a classless cop earning $47,000.00. You prize fought and that is even more classless. Most living in this neighborhood earn $65,000.00 or more and are in upper cooperate management or business owners. I am trying to be as light as I can.

Mary: (Mary grabs Jack's leg and tells him she can handle the situation.) Honey, please let me handle this and don't get worked up.

Jack: (Snaps to Mary while looking at Murdock.) No, he just told me my family isn't good enough. We will never accept an offer like yours. We don't want to return to New York. Were you the guy buying justice from Lt Gold? Well guess what, he was fired for corruption and justice is no longer for sale. Were you the guy who sent me this $300.00 to fix some fines on illegal dumping? (Jack throws the money in Murdock's face.) Well take your damn money because I'm not fixing those fines and if you don't straighten up, I'll fine you out of town. (Moving quickly with violent body language and screaming loudly.) Now pack up your paperwork and get the hell out of here. (Murdock quickly packs up and runs out of the room with Jack in hot pursuit and slams the door behind him. Jack turns with a smile.) Well we are wasting time, let's settle and get a house.

Scene Ten: A new Life.

Dave: (While the Bordowskis move in, Laura, Dave and Thomas Davidson plan on meeting their new neighbors.) Mom, that little girl is so beautiful, is that what an angel looks like?

Laura: Honey, I don't know. Would you like to meet the new neighbors?

Dave: Yes, I want to meet that little girl.

Laura: (As the three walk over and knock on the door, the two women introduce themselves to each other.) Hi, I'm Laura Davidson and these are my two boys, David and Tommy. Do you need any help moving in?

Mary: Hello, I'm Mary Bordowski, why don't the three of you come in and meet the family? (All are introduced and the kids play.)

Dave: Mrs. Bordowski, what is your little girl's name?

Laura: Can you introduce them?

Dave: Is your little girl an angel? (The adults laugh.)

Mary: Yes, she is an angel. Would you like to know her?

Dave: Yes, I would like to play with her.

Mary: Doreen, come over here and meet Dave, he is our neighbor from across the street.

Dave: Do you want to play outside?

Doreen: We can play in my back yard.

Mary: (The kids built sand castles out back and had a great time. The two ladies enjoyed getting to know each other and planned for the two men to meet that night after Bill's office hours.) Laura, come in and introduce me to your husband.

Laura: Mary, this is my husband, Bill; Bill, meet Mary.

Bill: Hello Mary, nice to meet you.

Mary: It's nice to meet you, too. Come out back and meet my husband Jack. (Mary introduces the two men.)

Jack: Would you like a beer and something to eat?

Bill: Yes, I'll take you up on both, thank you.

Jack: Tell me about this neighborhood.

Bill: You picked a very nice area to move into. The school district is great. There is also a lot of entertainment in the area.

Jack: A guy by the last name of Murdock tried to buy us out of the house at settlement. He didn't want me to take the job so bad he offered me $100,000.00 to resign and return to New York.

Bill: Mr. Murdock is one of those people who have nothing better to do than push his weight with his money. The police have visited my house over my dog barking and a few parties. We don't get along with them.

Jack: Murdock offered me money to fix fines for illegally dumping his chemical company does and I handed it back at settlement. I not only refused his offer, I chased him out of the room. Yes, he told me because I am a cop and a prize fighter that we don't fit this neighborhood. I'm the new Lieutenant in Middletown.

Bill: Does this mean my family won't be harassed due to the nuisance ordinances?

Jack: They're no nuisance laws in Middletown. Do you see the justice this money bought? That ended when Lieutenant Gold was fired and I was hired.

Bill: Glad to see a good cop in town. I hold nothing personal against cops; I just want to see fewer of them at my door with a complaint from the Murdock's. I know one cop that will be over in civilian clothing.

Jack: I'll or should I say we will be glad to attend.

Bill: How often do you fight and is it worth it?

Jack: I used to fight once a week and it was worth it because the prize money afforded us a nice down payment. This Sunday will be my last fight. It's a pain traveling back and forth from NYC. Now I have a good job and the house we want.

Mary: I have a letter from an old friend of yours. Tom Janzier, with a new rank beside his name, it looks like he has been promoted again. The letter is from Hawaii. Jack you have to read this and get back to him.

Jack: Tell me what you do with your spare time.

Bill: I joined Penn Manor Club. We camp, swim, water ski, fish, and anything you can imagine. You can hunt small game and there is a shooting range.

Jack: Can I go with you some time?

Bill: We will take your whole family as our guests on Sunday.

Jack: It will have to wait until next Sunday. I have my final fight this Sunday and I won't return on time. If I win I retire, if I lose I give up my crown. I think I will last five minutes and throw the fight. This way it is guaranteed I lose my crown and don't come back. The money has been great but I'm tired of mending my cuts and bruises.

Bill: Life like that can take a toll on you. If you stay with fighting, migraines and tremors can start up.

Jack: The migraines have already started.

Bill: It would be smart to get out as you planned.

Mary: I told you fighting wasn't any good for you. Do you have to go on Sunday? Why can't you just quit today?

Jack: Pride tells me to do the right thing. I have already called Ernie Dickens up and he will be my challenger. He is also going to choose gloves. This means I won't come home as ugly. I will try to last five minutes and throw the fight. Here I bring home some money. Ernie needs some money so he will get something he needs out of this. (Jack shows up and accepts challenge. When he lays no side bet Sully senses this is the end of Jack's crown.) Hello Sully, how is everything going?

Sully: Everything is fine; do you want to place a side wager on the fight?

Jack: Didn't bring any money with me. Who is the challenger?

Sully: Ernie Dickens says he will beat you and he wants a gloved fight.

Jack: So does everyone.

Ernie: So this is what you call a champ? I'll take him out. I already know the rules; I want a gloved fight and up close for the start.

Sully: (After equipment is on.) OK, guys, on the first clap get within four feet of each other with your dukes up. On the second clap you may open fire on each other. Are both of you ready? (Both answer yes and Sully claps the first time. He allows them to intimidate each other.)

Ernie: Are you ready to die, faggot?

Jack: Let's see what you've got, puss.

Sully: OK, guys, time to get it on. (Sully gives the second clap and they fire away.)

Scene Eleven: The final fight.

Jack: (Jack fires a left hook to Ernie's right eye. Ernie counters with a sharp left jab to Jack's right eye. The two dance for a bit occasionally firing a punch to the others face. The two tire of cat and mouse dancing and go toe to toe slugging as hard as they can to the other's body and face. Ernie proves to be faster than he looks. Jack gets in close and throws multiple hard punches to the body; Ernie winces in a lot of pain. Ernie launches a hard shot into Jack's stomach to back him away, then a combination to Jack's face and an upper cut that knocks Jack on his ass. Sully counts to six and waves the two on to fight. Jack starts to dance with Ernie. Then the two close in and fire a mad flurry of punches. Jack takes a sharp shot to the chin knocking him back a few steps. Jack steps back inside Ernie's reach and starts blowing his ribs out. Ernie doubles over and falls to the ground and receives an eight count. The two are waved on to fight. With four and a half minutes elapsed they begin to dance, Ernie lowers his right glove to cover the rib area and fires a left jab into Jack's face. Jack counters with a left to Ernie's already swelled right eye. With five minutes elapsed and Ernie teetering. Jack overhears the Union Rep say our whole department's money is on Ernie and it doesn't look good. Jack lowers his hands and takes a weak hook that knocks him on his ass. Sully moves in and counts to ten, a new champ is crowned. Jack shook hands with Ernie and the rest of the department. He then takes his money and goes home to a warm greeting from his wife.)

Mary: (Hugs and kisses Jack.) How's my champ. This is the last time I will have to cover up bruises, isn't it? Just think, you have a week to heal and should look good for your first day.

Jack: I intentionally allowed myself to be dethroned. I could have beaten Ernie but my promise to you meant too much and I am tired of traveling there.

Mary: Do you want to go to the lakes? Bill gave me directions and we can still catch the afternoon and later part of the day. Bill gave me a week's visitors pass.

Jack: I would like that; let's pack the kids up and go. I have five hundred dollars for you. It's time to have some fun. (The Bordowskis rent a tent and join the Davidson's who have had camp set up. Both families quickly set the Bordowskis tent up and the four older girls learned how to water ski and raft off the back of the Davidson's speed boat Little Lisa. The Davidson's also owned a row boat with a trolling motor. Later Bill showed Jack all six thousand acres of Penn Manor. The Bordowskis decide to spend a few pleasant days and relax before Jack starts work.) Mary, I would like to join for the rest of the year. Tomorrow, I want bass and eggs for breakfast and Bill said we could use the row boat with trolling motor any time we want.

Mary: (Mary notices there are lots of outhouses but she doesn't like using them.) Laura does the club have a bathroom? I don't like using the outhouse.

Laura: There are some bathrooms with showers at the clubhouse. I will take you there now.

Mary: Do you think the clubhouse is still open? How much does a family membership cost?

Laura: The office should still be open. We can stop in and talk to Joan to set things up.

Mary: Jack will love this. I can't wait to see his face. (Mary joins the lakes and surprises Jack when she gets back.)

Jack: What took you so long to go to the bathroom?

Mary: I did much more than go to the bathroom. I went to the clubhouse and joined the club with a basic family membership. This place is so nice I couldn't resist. It only cost $250.00 for the year.

Jack: (The two share a warm kiss.) I love you honey.

Mary: I love you too. It's time to start dinner. Did you want to start a fire and try your luck in the lakes with these worms?

Jack: Why not, we have hot dogs and hamburgers if I don't catch anything. (The only one of the girls interested in going fishing is Doreen. Jack hooks two bass that he helps Doreen reel in.)

Doreen: Daddy, these fish are so big. They will make a good dinner.

Jack: That's my fishing girl. I have to clean them to eat the fish; this is something that you shouldn't see. I'll bring you up to mommy. (After dinner a camp fire, lots of games and gabbing with the Davidson's into the late night hours, The Bordowski Family turns in. As the sun is coming up Mary wakes up horny. She wakes Jack up by pulling on his penis under the covers. Jack wakes up and begins kissing Mary's neck and massaging Mary's clitoris until she is hot, wet and ready for love. Mary turns on her side and inserts Jack's throbbing flesh inside of her hot, wet tunnel of love. As Jack softly strokes her Mary begins to moan so Jack covers her mouth.) SHHH! You'll wake everybody up.

Mary: (Aggravated but whispering.) Don't cover my mouth and nose, just kiss me honey. Keep stroking until you cum. We need to finish quickly, the girls are starting to stir. (Jack begins to get really excited and starts stroking harder. Mary begins to quiver from an intense orgasm. Mary strokes Jack's nuts softly until he cums. When they are finished Mary is still trembling from an intense orgasm.) Kiss me and hold me, I'm still having an orgasm.

Jack: (Whispers to Mary.) You're so bad.

Mary: (Whispers to Jack.) But that's when love is so good. (Before the kids get up, Mary and Jack exit the tent. Before the kids come out of the tent Mary whispers to Jack.) I haven't had enough of you. I'm so god damn horny I'm going to get nasty. Please come up with something quick.

Jack: (With a smile whispers.) This was your bright idea. I have it, we're going fishing. Danielle is in charge. We can satisfy this problem with two hours of fishing in the reeds.

Mary: Danielle is coming out of the tent.

Jack: Start for the boat, everything is loaded, all I have to do is tell Danielle she is in charge and the two small ones are not to be in the water.

Danielle: Dad, why can't we come?

Jack: Because mom and I have to catch breakfast and there isn't enough room in the boat. You are in charge, don't let the little ones in the water and we'll be back in a few hours.

Danielle: Mom and dad, why can't you catch fish right here, you did it yesterday.

Jack: (In a sharp tone.) Danielle, there are no fish here today.

Mary: (In a sharp tone.) Danielle, was there anything your father said that was unclear?

Jack: (After Danielle got the message the two lovers shove off for the reeds.)Let's go to where the high reeds and steep drop off are. There should be good cover for us and some good fishing.

Mary: What do you want to catch?

Jack: Something about 130 lbs, tall, brown hair and brown eyes. My feeling is that we got rushed to make love and didn't get enough of each other.

Mary: You're right, pull into the reeds. (Mary and Jack anchor the boat and begin kissing. Mary unbuttons her blouse and bra as Jack begins to touch her breasts softly and they begin French Kissing. Mary pulls Jack's zipper down and begins to softly pull on Jack's throbbing flesh. Jack begins softly sucking on Mary's right breast while working the nipple with his tongue. Jack begins to massage Mary's clitoris and she lay on the bottom of the boat quivering and moaning from an intense orgasm. After awhile she begins to suck Jack's penis, lies back and inserts him inside of her. The second she inserts him Mary groans loudly. Jack gently strokes Mary and kisses her with a probing tongue to keep her quiet. When Mary's orgasm is over they go fishing.) Jack, I love you so much.

Jack: I love you to. We have to go fishing and come home with something or the kids will know something is up.

Mary: (On her first cast.) Honey, I have something big.

Jack: Well look at the size of that big mouth bass. You may out fish me this morning. I don't want to stay out longer than another hour.

Mary: This is a keeper and will start breakfast.

Jack: Now I have a nice fish, one or two more and we will have enough. (The Bordowskis returned and had a bass and eggs breakfast. Jack and Bill took the Little Lisa and toured Van Sciver Lake for hours.)

Mary: Jack, did you read the letter from Tom Janzier. He called and said he will be landing in Phila. this evening and will be visiting his sister in Bristol for ten days. Tom left his sister's number.

Jack: I will call tonight and if you don't mind, see him tomorrow. (Jack calls Trudy Hastings.) Hello, Is this Trudy Hastings? My name is Jack Bordowski; I was wondering if you knew when Tom was coming in?

Trudy: Tom will land in Phila. tonight at 11:15 P M on Pan American 415. I'm so tired I wish I didn't have to make that drive.

Jack: Would you like to surprise him. I can drive you or get him myself.

Trudy: That would be great. I will come with you.

Jack: Honey, can I pick my friend Tom up at the airport tonight. I haven't seen him in about nine years.

Mary: Why not, you're home every night and deserve a night out.

Jack: I'll probably be late.

Mary: Just enjoy yourself.

Scene Twelve: The Seven Year Reunion.

Tom: Well how are the two of you doing? (Tom embraces both Trudy and Jack.) It's been such a long time. Let's get some drinks in the bar.

Jack: (With a smile.) What are you, a squid?

Tom: (The two buy a six pack at the airport. On the ride home, Tom pulls out a bottle of Jose Quervo and some shot glasses. Even though he is a cop, Jack starts drinking beer and doing shots while driving.) To a Seven Year Reunion with family and a great friend. Bottoms up, guys.

Jack: The last seven years in the Navy have been good to you for promotions. How have things gone in general?

Tom: (After a shot and some beer.) After that mess we had in Nam I straightened my life out by resigning my Army Commission and going Navy. The worst thing I had to do is go through forty-five days of cross training. I also got married three years ago.

Jack: Have you had any children?

Tom: I have a year old son and one on the way.

Jack: Tell me all about the places you have been stationed.

Tom: Although I've seen many ports, I have spent my entire Naval Career in Pearl Harbor, Hawaii.

Jack: Have you visited the Philippines and Australia?

Tom: Yes, I visited both three times. I married a Filipino girl. I love the freedom and great treatment I get. Her name is Wilma and she is the finest woman I've ever known, she takes care of my son, my house and me. Wilma also grants me the freedom I need to travel as long as I don't run. Officers need wives that represent them well to their command, the public and the admiral. (Tom proposes a toast to the women in each mans life and both toast.) Jack, tell me about your wife.

Jack: My wife is the finest woman I know. We have been married for eight years and are still going strong. I can talk to my wife about anything and have a clean house and great food on the table. We still make love often and I know I couldn't have made out better. I have six daughters that are all great girls. I will have to open our schedule up so you can meet Mary. Wait until you meet Mary and my girls; I know they will take to you. (Jack drops Tom and Trudy off and gets home about one.)

Tom: If possible can I meet your family tomorrow; I'm only in town for three days.

Jack: I will call tomorrow after I check with Mary. (The next morning.) Honey, can I bring an old friend over. Tom is only here for three days and is the type person you would take to.

Mary: I would like that. I have seen many letters from him and it is time to meet him. Let's set plans for seven o'clock so you have time to clean up after work and pick him up without rushing around.

Jack: (Gives Tom a quick call.) Hello Tom, it's me, we're on for tonight. I can pick you up about seven o'clock. My wife is going all the way. We will start out with crab stuffed mushrooms; the main course will be steak and lobster.

Tom: That will be great; I will get to meet your whole family. How are you feeling after last night? I haven't drunk like that in some time and my recovery is very slow. I will be all right by the time I see you.

Jack: My recovery has been very slow after ten drinks. By the way, my wife can't wait to meet the man I've spoken about the past seven or eight years.

Tom: I can hardly wait to meet your family. If you don't mind, I would like to pick up a housewarming gift and some flowers for your wife.

Jack: I don't mind, but tell me what got into you over the years?

Tom: I became a gentleman over the years and it has paid off. The women you saw pictures of me with weren't ladies, the woman I showed you a picture of last night is. Besides, the only way your wife will let me see you again is if she approves of me. That is the way things go when you're married. (Tom gets a beautiful brass piece for the front door with the Bordowski name on it and a beautiful bouquet of red roses for Mary.)

Jack: (In a joking manner.) Are you sure you aren't making a move on my wife.

Tom: Only for her approval.

Jack: (As the two enter the house, Jack introduces Tom to Mary and the kids.) Honey, this is Thomas Janzier, the gentleman I spoke so much of in Vietnam.

Mary: Pleased to meet you Tom. (Tom bears the gifts.) How nice, you didn't have to do that. (Mary is taken by Tom's good looks and gentlemanly way.)

Tom: Just some presents for a couple in a new home. Your husband is quite a man. He has a lot of character, a great heart, and without him I'm not alive. I couldn't imagine him married to a woman of any less character and goodness.

Mary: You have a lot of class in your choice of gifts and in your way.

Tom: I see Jack has married well. You have a beautiful home, family and a warm and friendly welcome. (Jack sees Mary taking to Tom but doesn't seem to care as they appear to have a lot in common.)

Mary: Tom where do you come from?

Tom: The historic District in Bristol. Are you familiar with it?

Mary: Are you speaking of Radcliffe Street? I love those old homes. Did you grow up near the wharf?

Tom: Yes, I grew up on the two hundred block of Radcliffe Street and spent a lot of time there. I understand they still have a beautiful fireworks display on the Fourth of July and New Year's Eve.

Mary: Where were you educated?

Tom: My elementary and middle school years were at Newtown Friends School. My high school years were for the most part at the George School but due to a few technical difficulties I finished up at Bristol High.

Mary: Your parents must have done well to send you to private school. The George School is known across the country for its academic standards. I understand they have a great exchange program.

Tom: My father was an investment banker for Fidelity Bank and a great business man. My sister Trudy and I wanted for nothing.

Jack: If the two of you don't mind, can I get either of you a drink or bowl of shrimp?

Mary: Why don't you get some champagne for the three of us? We should have a toast to two old friends getting together and meeting new friends. Honey, this one of the few friends you have that has anything in common with me. You were right that I would like him.

Jack: Honey, is it all right if I speak to Tom?

Mary: When I'm finished. Why don't you talk with us, you may find some things out about Tom you never knew.

Tom: Mary, where did you come from?

Mary: I'm born and raised in Rochester, New York. Like you I was raised in money. My father was a successful Neurologist who was rarely home. Between his practice, being on the Board of Directors, and lecturing nation wide he was almost never around. I had every toy imaginable and still felt alone. I was raised by my mother who was great to me but I never had any brothers or sisters. I love children so much I had six of them.

Tom: Did you go to private or parochial school?

Mary: I went to St. Ann's in a well to do section of Rochester with all the white bread girls and felt life was passing me by. My mother was a great girl and a lot of fun, but she could get stiff on the rules and prissiness. I was raised to be an example to the neighborhood. At times the pressure to look great was so great I felt like screaming.

Tom: We had a lot in common in our childhoods. I rebelled by fighting, drinking and doing drugs as a teenager. I was forced to join the military when I beat up a cop. I didn't think I would stay beyond one enlistment but I wound up loving the military and now I am a midline officer.

Mary: You have really come back in life. The armed forces have completely changed your life.

Jack: OK everybody, I have champagne and strawberries. Let's make a toast to permanent friendship.

Tom: Here, here, to a great and lasting friendship. (All Parties toast.)

Jack: Didn't you attend a course in communications around Long Island?

Tom: Yes, (With a smile.) when I passed through I saw a lot of signs to throw Rochester out of New York. Is there anything to that?

Mary: Yes, we aren't well liked because we have lots of money and flaunt it.

Jack: It goes a lot further than that. People in Rochester think they are above the rest and there was a state wide vote to throw Rochester out of New York.

Tom: (With a smile.)That must have been close? I know Rochester was kept.

Jack: A recount was needed but the state didn't want to lose a great university.

Mary: (With a smart tone.) Which way did your vote go, Jack?

Jack: (Laughing for a moment.) The way I vote is my business.

Mary: (With a tone.) Yes, but whether you get a hot meal or a warm bed to sleep in is my business.

Tom: (Holding back laughter.) Did I start something I shouldn't have? Should I leave?

Mary: Jack, I know you don't like my home town. Which way did you vote?

Jack: I voted to keep Rochester.

Mary: I'm certain you didn't, at least you said the right thing. (Mary gives Jack a nice kiss off the lips to let Jack know the contest is over.) It is starting to get late and I have enjoyed the evening and company. Jack, if you get back at a reasonable hour, you will have a warm bed, but you will have to earn your hot breakfast.

Jack: I'll be back in about an hour, in a warm bed and will earn my hot breakfast.

Mary: Tom, it was nice meeting you and you are welcome any time you are in the area.

Tom: It was a pleasure to meet you and the family of the man that saved my life.

Jack: (In the car.) My wife really enjoyed your company. I can have you over any time you are in the area; give me a ring.

Tom: You have a wonderful family. I will be heading home tomorrow afternoon.

Jack: Will you need a ride?

Tom: No, Trudy will take me to the airport. Try to stay in a bit more contact.

(The two exchange numbers and say goodbye. Both return to warm receptions from their wives.)

Scene Thirteen: A Visit from Bad Company.

Mary: (After Jack goes to work Mary answers a knock on the door.) Hello, I'm Mary Bordowski, what can I do for you?

Eileen: Hello, I'm Eileen Murdock and my two children Linda and Brenda. We tried to meet you earlier this summer but no one was home most of the time.

Mary: We joined Penn Manor Lakes. I take my children down there with Laura Davidson and her two boys almost every day. Come in, let's have some cake and coffee and get to know each other a little.

Eileen: I hear your husband is a police Lieutenant in Middletown. Where did you come from?

Mary: We came in from Brooklyn New York. My husband was a city cop for the last seven years.

Eileen: Did your husband belong to the military? Many of them join the police force after their careers.

Mary: My husband was in the infantry in Vietnam. He only saw action for four months. What does your husband do?

Eileen: He owns Bridgeway Chemicals. He provides Rohm and Haas chemical compounds and ships them to Bristol. My husband and I come from a long line of entrepreneurs. My husband's father owned his own chemical lab and my father owned his own architectural firm. My father was hardly ever home.

Mary: As far as a father who was hardly ever home I had the same sort of thing going on. My father is a successful neurologist and President of the Board of Directors at Tri County Hospital in Rochester New York. My father is The Medical Director and teaches medical courses. He also travels nation wide to lecture on different neurological diseases such as MS. My grandmother suffered horribly from it before she died.

Eileen: I notice you have a very nice chess set. Do you play?

Mary: Yes, my husband and I occasionally lock up into a contest.

Eileen: Could we play a game while we get to know each other?

Mary: Why not, since Jack assumed his duties three months ago, we haven't had time to play. We can send the kids outback while we play. (Mary introduces the kids and sends them outback to play while Mary and Eileen got to know each other over coffee, cake and chess.) Eileen, since you are visiting, you should get first move.

Eileen: Thank you, I can tell you were raised in social grace. Tell me a bit about your educational background.

Mary: My whole educational background was in the parochial and private school sector. My elementary school years were at St. Ann's and my high school years were in Log College. A well known private school in Rochester. College was a little different. I attended the University of Rochester for two and a half years and transferred to NYU for several good reasons. I wanted to experience city life and I had to stop my family from running my entire life.

Eileen: I was raised in California and went to Catholic School during my grade school years. I received my undergraduate, graduate and PHD at UCLA. My undergraduate degree was in accounting. My graduate degree was in chemistry as well as my PHD. I met my husband at a chess tournament at UCLA and we fell in love right away. I knew I would be leaving home when he asked me to marry him but I knew there was a bright future in store. Bob held the collegiate chess crown for three years before he was beaten by the first female ever to win the crown. That really aggravated him. Sometimes he still shows as a male supremacist. Today I handle the office work and company books. (Eileen is amazed at Mary's ability to take a lot of breaks and play effectively.) Tell me how you met your husband.

Mary: It was by odd circumstances. Jack was my fiancés best friend. My fiancés name was Jay Merriweather and the reason I dated Jay is because Jack never made a move on me. When Jay and I broke up, Jack was there for me. We started dating when things straightened out for me.

Eileen: When did you start to play chess and how good is your husband?

Mary: I began playing with my parents about the age of five. It was one of my father's favorite things to do with me when he was home. My father stopped competing when he went into practice. He missed the game so much he turned me into a good player. My mother is also a great chess player who has put my father in his place on more than one occasion. Both are to the intellectual side and love mind games. I joined a chess league that met twice a week for several years. I reached the top competing in high school and college. Jack competed in college and reached the top five of one hundred players. His first loss came to me. It was a three hour struggle that went back and forth. I liked him so much I hated beating him and Jack beats me about half the time we play. My husband is as brilliant a man in life as he is on the chess board. (Mary wins game one in a two hour struggle.) Looks like we have check mate Eileen.

Eileen: Looks like you're right; could we play another?

Mary: Yes, the last game was so good. You will get the first move. Tell me when you started to play.

Eileen: I started playing pretty young myself. I was seven years old and I was taught by my mother. Chess is truly a game of the elite. I competed at a country club we belonged to and won my first tournament at the age of twelve. I was a five year reigning champ. I competed at UCLA and came in the top three players but never won a tournament. My husband won three national titles and was beaten by the first woman collegiate chess champion Mary Carrington. A defeat he didn't take well. He is a sexist who can't take losing anything to a woman. At times he can be hard to handle but I'm used to him. (Mary looks at the clock and sees that Jack will be home in about a half hour and throws the game by taking her finger off a move that puts her in check mate.) Looks like I win this one. Could we play a rubber match at my house? How does 11:00 A.M.sound?

Mary: Tomorrow I will bring something to eat. Do you like shrimp cocktail? I will bring that for us and cup cakes for the kids.

Eileen: That will be great for our rubber match.

Jack: (When he gets home Jack hears about two new friends from Dallas who is the first to greet him coming in the door.) Well, how is my little girl?

Dallas: I'm doing fine daddy. We met two new friends today, Linda and Brenda Murdock.

Jack: Hi honey, how did your day go?

Mary: I had a decent day, I met Eileen Murdock.

Jack: Is that the Murdock Family down the street?

Mary: Yes, she has two very nice daughters Linda and Brenda. All the children played out back while Eileen and I played chess and talked about our backgrounds. She is nice, but I got this air of one upsmanship until I beat her in the first of two games of chess. I threw the second game because I didn't know how you would react if she was here when you got home.

Jack: The only way I would have blown up is if I saw Bob Murdock or a criminal in the house. I take it she is a lady.

Mary: Yes, she is very well raised. She has a good educational background and comes from a business family.

Jack: I would watch my step with her. Honey, do yourself a favor and call Laura before you go over there because I don't trust them or this gesture of friendship. With a husband like Bob, she could be trying to find things to start war with us.

Mary: I will call Laura and see what I'm getting into.

Jack: Do you think things will go all right tomorrow?

Mary: The kids should have a good time. The adults will eat shrimp cocktail while the kids will have cup cakes. Everything will go OK until I beat her on the chess board. I would like to play her husband again, he is the guy I beat for the championship in 1969. He was so arrogant when we met and so angry when he lost the match he didn't shake my hand at the start or finish of the match.

Jack: What type of man is he?

Mary: Bob is a sexiest pig. He wouldn't shake my hand and told me chess isn't for women. I beat him in a hotly contested three and a half hour match. He was showing the same arrogance at settlement. I almost wish you pounded him. (After dinner Mary calls Laura to see what happened between the Davidsons and Murdocks.) Hi Laura, it's Mary.

Laura: How are you doing, we haven't spoken for a few days.

Mary: I have been shopping for school clothes for the kids. I also got a surprise visit from your next door neighbor.

Laura: Watch her, Eileen is a witch. She started with friendly visits to our house, all she wants to see if you have pets or noisy kids. The next move is to invite you over to their house and they try to find out personal information and begin to complain to the police and local politicians about you. They complained about our dog, parties in the daytime and a loud fight Bill and I had. Watch what you let them see. Don't give any personal information.

Mary: I will have my eye on her tomorrow. If you're up for a visit, I will probably be open tomorrow afternoon. (Mary talks to Jack about tomorrow and what was said and done.) Well, Laura told me to watch what I say or do with her and not to hand out personal information.

Jack: (In a calm tone.) Tell me what you showed and told her.

Mary: I showed her the entire downstairs and back yard. She saw we have a dog and met all of the kids.

Jack: Nothing will go drastically wrong there. They may start on the dog barking. I will notify everyone I handle all complaints from the Murdocks. Tell me about your conversation.

Mary: We spoke of our family backgrounds for all sides of the family. I really didn't go deep into your side.

Jack: The only thing he can use against me is that I used to fight for money. Watch for snobbery and for her to use us not fitting the neighborhood because I'm a cop. Let me know how tomorrow goes and make sure you beat that bitch convincingly.

Mary: I need to pick up shrimp cocktail and my baking needs for tomorrow. (Mary prepares the food and brings the girls over the Murdock's House.)

Scene Fourteen: A Visit to the Snake Pit.

Eileen: (With a bright smile.) Hello, come on in. We have been waiting for you. Bring the food into the kitchen. I have cake and coffee is brewing. If you and the girls want something cold to drink, we have soda, lemonade, and several juices. Let's go out back and get the kids started so we can play chess.

Mary: I love the size of your back yard. You have a nice in ground pool, swing set and sand box. Let's push the kids on the swings and in a few minutes we can talk and play chess. (Both swing the kids and get them started.) It looks like the kids are having fun.

Eileen: Let's go in. I may have another surprise visitor.

Mary: Anybody I know or should get to know?

Eileen: Yes, and he is waiting to meet you socially rather than on the chess board.

Mary: Who could that be?

Eileen: My husband Bob. He is worried about the bad impression he left on you at settlement and at the chess tournament in 1969. (Bob is waiting in the kitchen.) Bob this is Mary Bordowski.

Bob: (Shakes Mary's hand.) Pleased to meet you. You look so familiar. Do you mind my asking what your maiden name is?

Mary: My maiden name is Carrington. We did meet in the college chess finals at UCLA. (Mary wonders if Bob is still angry about losing to a woman.) That has to go back eight or nine years ago.

Bob: I hope you will accept my apology for my arrogance at settlement and the finals. You may not believe this, but I am a better person than that.

Mary: (Mary shakes his hand again and accepts his apology.) You seem to have come a long way Bob.

Bob: Back in 1969 I felt like a jerk losing to a woman because women weren't supposed to be competitive with men in anything. Today there isn't anything a man can do that a woman can't. My wife handles many of our contracts, company books and office paperwork. She also does a great job taking care of the house and family.

Mary: I'm so happy you've changed over the years. I would like to apologize for my husband's anger.

Bob: That's all right, I could have been lighter. You have six beautiful girls. Do you think your husband will forgive me?

Mary: Thank you for your compliments on my family. As far as my husband goes, he forgives everything in time.

Bob: I have a pressing engagement; it was nice to meet you. I have to be going.

Eileen: Shall we begin our rubber match?

Mary: Let's get the food and drink on the table and begin right away.

Eileen: You look so nice today. I like the sun dress you are wearing.

Mary: I always try to look good. My parents stressed always look your best. Since you won the last game the first move is yours. (The girl's play a conservative game for the first thirty minutes until Eileen gets verbally aggressive knocking the Davidsons.)

Eileen: How is that snit Laura doing? I really don't like her and her husband Bill, or those two obnoxious boys of hers, Dave and Tommy. Between them and that nasty dog Angel always barking, the neighborhood is on its way down.

Mary: (Defensive and slightly annoyed tone.) Hey wait a minute, Laura and I are good friends. The boys have a lot of energy, but are not obnoxious. That dog is rarely out barking and is harmless.

Eileen: What is your opinion of Bill? When is the doctor going to grow up and drop the noisy motorcycle? Isn't it about time he gets in a practice?

Mary: Bill is a handsome and intelligent man. He is already in practice and I predict will be very successful when he gets his own practice. (Mary bates Eileen into a move for check mate within fifteen minutes of Eileen mouthing off.) I believe this move is check mate. You should have left your king covered.

Eileen: (In disgust, Eileen cuts the visit short and issues a warning.) We can swing the kids for half an hour and we then have to be going. To be friends with this family you will have to drop your friendship with the losers next door and your husband will have to bring justice back our way.

Mary: (With an aggravated tone.) I doubt either will happen. We are very friendly with the Davidsons and my husband will never sell justice.

Eileen: (With a nasty tone.) I can plainly see we won't be friends.

Mary: (With a nasty tone.) If you're as good a friend as you are a chess player, you won't be any kind of friend at all. The girls are enjoying themselves; I hope you won't put a stop to that. I certainly won't take your manipulation and poor conduct toward me out on your girls.

Eileen: (With a nasty tone.) That was put very bluntly.

Mary: (A nasty tone.) You were nasty to me and friends of mine.

Eileen: I will allow your kids to play with mine, but I want minimal contact with you and your husband. I have to tell you I have a lot of places to be. You and the kids have to be moving on.

Jack: (Smiling when he gets home and sitting down to dinner.) Honey, how did your visit to the Murdock residence go?

Mary: Very well, just as it appeared Bob Murdock had grown up with his views on women, he married a hatchet woman to do his dirty work.

Jack: What did Eileen have to say?

Mary: She wasn't very kind to the Davidsons and she wanted to know if you would bring justice back their way. I told her that we wouldn't drop our friendship with the Davidsons and my husband won't bring justice back their way. I told her the kids can play together but the adults won't be friends. Please don't be angry if you see the Murdock girls over. After checkmating Eileen in about forty-five minutes, I bluntly told her off.

Scene Fifteen: The Battle to Box

Jack: Good work, I won't mind the Murdock girls over. (We skip to 1984 and the Bordowski Family reputation is high. Mary is on the PTA while Jack is the Senior Lieutenant. Jack greets two new people from New York to the Middletown Police. Lieutenant Carlos Castillo and Sargent Virginia Lopez. Doreen learns how to box at the age of ten. At the dinner table Jack tells the family the good news and that he will also head the juvenile division.) Honey, I was asked to run the Pal League for boys and girls that want to box and wrestle. This is the first year girls are allowed to compete in combative sports in Middletown.

Mary: Some of the news is good. I don't mind you teaching these things to boys, but these sports are not for females.

Jack: The girls have it better than the boys; we will have judo to offer with the new transfer coming in from New York. Doreen, you and I have seen her box, her name is Virginia Lopez.

Doreen: Dad, can I come with you? Even though my favorite fighter is Sandra O'Shea, Virginia is a great fighter. I will learn a lot.

Mary: Doreen, you are only ten years old. Jack, I don't want her there nor do I like it when she is play fighting with you.

Doreen: I turn eleven in six weeks and I want to learn how to fight. I have a chance to learn from one of the best.

Mary: Doreen, fighting is for boys and men.

Jack: That isn't so, since the seventies women have taken up self defense.

Deirdre: Mom, let them go, Doreen is the only one of us you allowed to bond with dad.

Danielle: Wow dad, I wish you would do something like that for the rest of us.

Dallas: (With a smartass tone.) Yeah dad, you do everything for Dory. Sometimes I just want to smack her.

Mary: Girls, that's enough. Doreen, what makes you want to learn how to fight?

Doreen: I want to know how to defend myself and I want to box or wrestle competitively.

Mary: Why don't you pick out a female sport like field hockey, basketball, or soft ball? Why don't you try for the school play or chorus? Do something girls do.

Doreen: Is that what you did when you won the collegian chess championship? At that time women supposedly weren't chess players.

Mary: That was different because chess is nonviolent.

Doreen: I still want to be the best female wrestler and boxer ever. I want to compete to know where I stand. That sounds a lot like you mom. The need to know just how good we are is one thing the Bordowski and Carrington families have in common.

Mary: Why male contact sports?

Doreen: Because I'm good at them. I'm going with dad whether you like it or not.

Mary: What do you want from me?

Doreen: I would like you to say it's all right.

Mary: I never will.

Doreen: Then dad's backing will have to be enough. I still love you mom but a girl has to do what a girl has to do. Dad when you go I will be coming with you.

Mary: (With a stern voice and face.) Doreen, we will pick this up without fighting after dinner.

Doreen: Mom, it probably won't make a difference, but I'll agree to a talk. (Turns to dad.) I want to learn how to box and wrestle. This is my chance to get competitive. I hope some girls sign up. If not, will you still let me compete?

Jack: As long as Virginia can find fights for you, you can compete. I can't allow you to fight a boy. The state won't allow that at this time. Even if no other girls sign up Virginia can work with you and show you many of the different speed and punching drills.

Doreen: What are speed drills?

Jack: When two people throw light fast punches at each others chests. The objective is to block as many of the opponent's punches as is possible while you are also trying to hit your opponent in the chest. Two heroes of yours. Brenda Lott and Sandra O'Shea used to work out like this both before and during their pro careers.

Doreen: What happened to them? Both were Pennsylvania's number one girls and one was a national champion.

Jack: So the story goes, Brenda got married; she wanted to be a housewife and mother. Brenda held the national championship for the Women's Boxing Federation which is a league that rivals the WBA. As far as Sandra O'Shea goes, she still is good friends with Brenda Lott and was trained by Brenda at first. Sandra fought the still reigning champ, Nita Fernandez for the championship and lost in split decision. Sandy is taking her time getting ready for a rematch later this year. The date has not been announced. Sandra O'Shea said if she loses she will join the Navy as an officer and see the world. With Nita Fernandez avoiding a fight with Virginia Lopez, it will be awhile before anyone from this state challenges for the WBF title.

Doreen: Dad, does the WBA box the WBF? Do you think I could go pro at seventeen?

Jack: I would back that if that is what you really want.

Doreen: Do you think I'm as good as Sandra O'Shea or Brenda Lott?

Jack: I know you can be. To be great at boxing you have to work at it every day. You will have to eat right and exercise every day. Your workouts will include footwork, punching drills and defense. If you wish to box and wrestle it will be tough. You may just want to pick the one you like best.

Doreen: Will you let me wrestle a boy? I've already beaten two in wrestling at recess.

Jack: The answer is no for two good reasons. This state doesn't allow for contact sports between men and women and I don't think men and women should be physically fighting in any way.

Doreen: OK dad, let's hope some girls show up for both. I will concentrate on boxing, but I will learn to wrestle because I could be one of those great WWF Divas.

Mary: Doreen, I would like to talk to you in the kitchen.

Doreen: (Exits the table.) All right mom, I'll be right in.

Dallas: I finally get a word or two in. Dad, since you are in charge of the juvenile division, does this mean that I get to do what I want and can I get people I don't like in trouble?

Jack: (With a loving playful smile and tone.) No, what it does mean is that you need to keep a lower profile or I'll have to straighten you out.

Dallas: (Smiles at dad and blows him a kiss.) I love you too dad.

Mary: (As Doreen walks into the kitchen, Mary uses a soft tactful voice.) Doreen, I didn't mean to pick a fight with you about the boxing but you know how I feel about fighting. I don't even like it for boys and grown men. I have even had it out with your father about watching that garbage with you on TV. Please think hard about what I've said and don't do it. Girls don't look right with black eyes, broken noses, bloody noses or bruises on their cheeks. Please be mommy's little girl and don't fight

Doreen: Mom, I want to be one of those girls who bring women's boxing in as a big time sport. Despite people watch men's boxing way more than women, we can get a wider following if more women box. I want to do for boxing in the future what you did for women playing collegian chess.

Mary: Honey, I would rather see you use your head to get women recognized than your fists or learning how to struggle on a mat. Please take the next four weeks to think about that. I don't want this to break into an argument between you and I. Give me a kiss and take the next few weeks to a month to think about it.

Doreen: (Gives mom a kiss off the cheek and joins Jack and her sisters in the living room.) Dad, even though mom doesn't want me fighting, I will be there with you when the PAL League starts.

Jack: Hopefully you didn't have an argument with your mother. (Gives Doreen a hug.)

Doreen: (Snuggles up to Jack and watches TV.) No, she tried to talk me out of boxing calmly but it won't work. I love you, daddy.

Jack: I love you too. (Doreen falls asleep next to dad and Jack carries her to bed. Four weeks later Doreen and Jack leave for the police station and pulls into the parking lot to a surprise.)

Scene Sixteen: The Beginning of a Successful Career.

Jack: Well, we have a good number of cars; hopefully there will be some girls who want to learn to defend themselves. Oh my God, looks like a fair amount of girls signing up. There is Sgt. Virginia Lopez who will be your instructor.

Doreen: This is going to be great day.

Jack: Sgt. Lopez is our most proficient at self defense. She knows judo, boxing and wrestling.

Doreen: Is she the best girl at hand to hand combat?

Jack: She isn't just the best woman, she is better than the men too.

Doreen: Do you think she could beat you?

Jack: I don't know. I boxed her for one light contact round and she beat me by three contacts. You will find that speed means at least as much as strength in a fight. Fighting comes down to a number of factors whether in the ring or on the street: You must deliver your offense with speed and power, have the ability to take a punch, and the ability to protect yourself when the other person is bringing the fight to you. In a well matched fight you will be tested by your opponent. People who can throw a punch but can't take one generally lose. When you are here Sgt. Lopez will teach you everything you need to know. I will work with you at home if you like. To stay with this there are several things you must remember. When it comes to your mother who is worried, you are not to argue with her. I will handle that area. Second, you are never to hit one of your sisters. Last but not least, you are not to let your grades slip.

Doreen: I know I can hold up to those things.

Jack: Let's go see who is here and I'll introduce you to Sgt. Lopez. Looks like you're in luck and some girls came to learn and compete. The gym is matted and ready. Virginia looks free, let me introduce you. Sgt. Lopez, now that we aren't on the clock, may I be informal and call you Virginia?

Sgt. Lopez: Yes, you can do that on the clock too as long as Chief Harris isn't around.

Jack: Virginia, this is my daughter Doreen. She wants to learn boxing and wrestling. Doreen, this is Sgt. Virginia Lopez.

Sgt. Lopez: So nice to meet you Doreen.

Doreen: It's nice to meet you too.

Sgt. Lopez: You are a very pretty and a nice young lady. I bet you take after your father in the ring and on the mats.

Jack: I still remember you defeated me as the quickest in the ring.

Sgt. Lopez: Yes, but that was only by a few contacts and a stroke of luck that you came up to throw a power punch at me which was side stepped and allowed me to slip inside. Otherwise things would have been quite different.

Jack: Believe it or not, I didn't mind losing to a conditioned woman. It was the most competitive speed drill I have ever had. I know my daughter is in great hands and I must meet my students. Doreen, listen to whatever Virginia tells you.

Sgt. Lopez: Girls, the first thing I need to do is introduce myself. I am your instructor Sgt. Virginia Lopez. I want this to be a relaxed and informal atmosphere so you are comfortable with me. Please just call me Virginia. I teach and compete in professional boxing and amateur wrestling and judo. Now, I must find out what all of you wish to learn. I also need to learn all of your names and whether you wish to learn to defend yourselves and who wants to compete.

Denise Castillo: (After raising her hand.) Is there a difference?

Sgt. Lopez: Yes, if you are going to compete you must stay in shape on an everyday basis. I run at least one mile per day and one hundred pushups and sit-ups per day. I have to stay in shape because I box professionally. I don't do as much judo or wrestling but I participate at the amateur level and represent our country in the Olympics and some amateur meets on the intramural police team. It is always very exciting to be part of a team event. Work always covered me with leave so I could go or took the time without pay. When I wrestled for the US I took second place. I also won two matches in judo before being defeated. I had a great time. If you are going to compete in contact violent sports like these you must accept the fact you will be hurt. Remember, learning how to fight is not for everybody and should not be how you settle your differences. Before we do anything, I need a show of hands. How many want to box? (All ten raise their hands. Four wanted to wrestle and one wanted to learn judo.) Since everybody wants to learn boxing we will start there first. Now I must teach you to wrap your hands. We will work on the heavy bag first. We will work on hitting a big bag first. Then I will show you speed punching drills without punching in the face. Let's get our hands wrapped and gloves on. (While instructing how to hit the heavy bags Sgt. Lopez notices only Doreen and Denise don't need help. While watching Doreen and Denise hit the heavy bag.) Wow, what did that bag ever do to the two of you? I will have the two of you to assist me in showing these young ladies how to throw a punch. Both of you must promise me you won't make fun of anybody in the learning stages and that you will be patient. I will need the two of you helping me so we can work on the big bags and speed bags. (Doreen and Denise took a student apiece and showed them the proper technique of punching the bag. At the end of an hour, the girls had a good workout. Four girls remained after the speed drills to learn wrestling and judo. Donna Riser, you do want to learn judo, don't you? For today you and I will use this period to double up. Then I will privately instruct you at least two to three times a week. Some of the throws and holds may help you with wrestling and if you stay with judo, I will find you at lease two matches a month like boxing and wrestling and if you want it, I will find you a match per week. This is one sport I can't get enough of. It's time to pair up and I will show you some basic moves. (After a half an hour of working out.) It is getting late, who wants to have a match? (Denise and Doreen raise their hands.) OK girls; let's get to the center of the mat. (As Sgt. Lopez blows the whistle to begin, both girls struggle to take each other to the mat. As the girls go to the mat they roll around five times until Denise gets a firm hold on Doreen for a three point takedown. Doreen breaks loose and reverses Denise for two points. As Denise breaks Doreen's hold the two struggle on the mat for control and roll around three times until play is stopped for being too near the edge of the mat. Since Doreen was in trouble she had to assume the bottom position. As the whistle blows to resume action, Denise tries to pull Doreen's close arm out and lifts her close leg. Doreen counters by rolling into Denise who can't hold on to her. Both girls shake loose of each other and get back to their feet. Denise bull rushes Doreen and as Doreen lands on her back she gets her knees rolled up into Denise's stomach and flips Denise on her back. Doreen gets on top of and pins Denise for the win.) That was a great match. The rest of you girls should take note of all the moves that were used.

Denise: That was a heck of a move to win the match. Where did you learn that?

Doreen: I learned from my father who wrestled in high school. You really know what you're doing on the mat. Where did you learn?

Denise: I learned from my father and brother. (In a snooty and challenging tone.) I know more moves than you but you beat me to the punch with strength and knowing how to neutralize everything I did. Bet I could beat you at boxing or wrestling if I put everything into what I was doing.

Doreen: (In a stern voice.) We can settle this in class when sparring starts. Wrestling we can settle next week also or when classes become several times a week. Please don't tell me I was lucky to beat you. Denise, you didn't look for the obvious move.

Denise: (Getting loud and challenging.) I had you most of the match and you beat me on one good move so you were lucky.

Doreen: (In a cool but snotty tone.) I wrestled to your ability and all beating you took was one good move. I will tell you it was you who was lucky. I let you look good.

Denise: (Loud and nasty.) Oh yeah, we'll settle this next week.

Sgt. Lopez: (In a serious manor.) Girls that will be quite enough. You can only wrestle if I am officiating the event. The two of you learned quickly and looked good but your comments lacked sportsmanship. Part of sportsmanship is accepting losing. In other words you must learn to lose as gracefully as you win. Next week the two of you will pair up with other girls. (The rest of the day Doreen and Denise paired up with other girls to show them moves and went home very tired from a big workout.)

Jack: (Back to the start of class.) OK guys lets get to know each other by name. I am Lt. Jack Bordowski; I will be overseeing the whole program for boxing and wrestling. I am a boxing instructor and Lt. Hellings is our wrestling instructor. I will assign some of the better students to help out this week and will get another instructor for each sport next week. (The boys split off into boxing and wrestling and went with their instructors. Jack calls the name Caesar Castillo.) Caesar, are you related to Lt. Carlos Castillo?

Caesar: Yes, he is my father.

Jack: Your father is one of the finest cops and men I have ever met.

Caesar: Thank you Lt Bordowski.

Jack: I need a show of hands. How many want to compete and how many just want to learn self defense? (Jack counts 16 hands of boys who want to compete and only four hands that want to learn to defend themselves.) We have enough to start a Middletown Boxing Team. Our station doesn't have a team in the PAL League. Before we begin to spar, I want to see what everybody has by having everybody hit a bag for a few moments. Let's get our hands wrapped and put our gloves on. Caesar, would you begin by hitting the heavy bag a few moments.

Scene Seventeen: Jack Picks an Assistant Coach and Team Captain

Caesar: Yes Lt. Bordowski, I would be happy to lead off.

Jack: (While watching Caesar.) Wow, you hit that bag as though you have been doing this for years. You carry a great rhythm and footwork. OK that is enough. I will quickly look at each boxer and evaluate whether you need to be worked with or not. All right, in my rounds I see eight people who will be starting from scratch. I will have more people to help out next week. If not, I will pull some of our better fighters to instruct. Our beginners will stay with me and practice their technique in a minute. I will set the rest of you up on the speed bags. (After a hard workout Jack calls everybody together and explains that things will change next Saturday.) OK guys, we have a month before we start competing. We won't meet again until Saturday morning at nine. After that the gym will be open nightly for workouts. If you are a serious boxer, you should be here every day for at least an hour or two. Our first meet is in early September. I will see all of you next Saturday. (The next day at work.) Lt. Castillo, talk to me for a minute.

Lt. Castillo: What is up Lt. Bordowski?

Jack: I just wanted to talk to you about your son. He is a great boxer and a gentleman. If you don't mind I would like to name him team captain. I would like to see if you would like to assist in coaching. There are twenty boys and eight really need to be worked with from scratch. I feel you and your son have a lot to offer. What do you say?

Lt. Castillo: (With a big smile and handshake.) I would be pleased to help train those young men. Hopefully we can get a good team trained. When do we start competing?

Jack: In four weeks. What I would like to do is work with the young men with less ability for the first thirty minutes, and then have everyone work together. If you like, you and I can switch back and forth with the young men who would need work. We should work out a plan between us by next Saturday.

Lt. Castillo: May I tell my son of your plans for him and can he sit in when we talk?

Jack: Yes, he is a sharp young man, bring him with you. It's time to clock on and be cops. We should be meeting early this week, what night is good for you?

Lt. Castillo: I will not be free until Wednesday. Is 7:00PM sounding good?

Jack: We will meet at my house at 7:00PM on Wednesday. (Jack answers the door Wednesday.)

Scene Eighteen: Deirdre Meets Her First Love.

Jack: Come in gentlemen. If you don't mind, I would like to go on a first name basis. I will introduce you to my wife. Mary, this is my sidekick and friend Lt. Carlos Castillo and his son Caesar.

Mary: Come in gentlemen, I have prepared stuffed mushrooms. I also have pick and peel shrimp. For the men I have beer and an assortment of things in the liquor cabinet. Caesar, we have soda and juice for you. If anyone doesn't like what we have, I can cook hotdogs and hamburgers. I will leave you gentlemen to talk.

Lt. Castillo: Your wife is beautiful and a great hostess.

Jack: She came up very well to do. Now we shouldn't take long to make a plan. I have already asked Chief Harris for seven day a week access to the gym and he approved it. I want to take charge of the kids who need a lot of work. I will be rotating in when we all meet together. We can take shifts with these kids but I have a special place in my heart for people who get picked on and want to learn how to defend themselves. We may get a few good fighters out of this bunch. One of the big things we must make sure of is that no one is being laughed at or picked on. That includes in the locker room. Caesar that is some of where you come in. You will be in with your father helping out organizing workouts. By the time sparring starts, hopefully I will have the kids that want to spar up to speed. The kids who just want to learn how to defend themselves can watch or head home. Hopefully some of them will want to compete.

Lt. Castillo: This sounds great to me.

Caesar: I love it. I can hardly wait until Saturday. Tell me Lt. Bordowski, when do we start competing with other teams?

Jack: We begin to compete with other teams in four weeks. Light sparring will begin next Saturday. Let me introduce you to my daughters. They are watching An Officer and A Gentleman.

Caesar: I know Deirdre a little. How many daughters do you have?

Jack: I have six daughters, only two are in the living room.

Caesar: I will be glad to meet them.

Caesar: (As the two enter the front room.) Doreen and Deirdre meet Caesar Castillo, Caesar, meet my daughters Doreen and Deirdre.

Doreen: Come in and join us.

Deirdre: I already know you from algebra and biology. I had no idea that you were Lt. Castillo's son.

Doreen: I met you at boxing today. You really know how to work a bag.

Caesar: I can't wait to start working out at the gym every night. That starts next Monday. Your father just got that approved. I can hardly wait to start.

Deirdre: Aren't you dating Bonita Siaz?

Caesar: For about a month, I ended that a few days ago.

Deirdre: What did you end everything for?

Caesar: Bonita said the wrong thing to several people. One of them was my mother and the other was a fellow football player which got me into a fist fight. I am at early workouts for football and PAL Boxing. I may quit football because I like boxing better and it leads to a schedule conflict. Bonita likes to see her man fight for her.

Deirdre: Was that a first time?

Caesar: No, last month I got into a fight in school over her. My parents restricted me for two weeks. I'm lucky my parents don't hit.

Deirdre: It looks like the two houses share that in common. (Deirdre whispers to Doreen.) Could you move to the rocking chair so Caesar can sit on the couch and talk to me? He is such a fox.

Doreen: (Whispering with a chuckle.) Deirdre has a boyfriend. (Doreen moves to the rocking chair.)

Caesar: (Sits on the end of the couch.) How far through the movie are you?

Deirdre: About the first half hour. Why don't you move closer so we can share the popcorn and talk? (The two start talking to each other and smiling. After a half hour or so the two start holding hands. By the end of the night Caesar asks Deirdre out to a movie Friday night and takes her number.)

Lt. Castillo: I'm afraid it's time to go. Thank you for asking my son and me to help out. Caesar, it's time to go.

Deirdre: I wish you could stay longer.

Caesar: I will save you a seat on the back of the bus tomorrow. Look for me as you get on the bus.

Deirdre: OK I will see you tomorrow.

Jack: (After the Castillo's leave.) Deirdre, do you know Caesar?

Deirdre: Yes, we ride the same bus and we have algebra and biology together.

Doreen: (Cutting Deirdre off.) Dad, Deirdre will be Caesar's new girlfriend. She gave him our number. They want to go to the movies next Friday and will sit together on the bus tomorrow. She even held his hand on the couch.

Deirdre: (Jack begins laughing. Deirdre shouts loudly.) Shut up Doreen.

Doreen: (With an annoying smile at Deirdre.) Deirdre's got a boyfriend, Deirdre's got a boyfriend.

Deirdre: (Yelling at Jack.) Make her shut up for God's sake.

Jack: Doreen that will be enough.

Doreen: Deirdre's got a boyfriend, Deirdre's got a boyfriend.

Jack: Doreen, please let your sister alone. Don't start on the two of them on the bus. By the way Deirdre, he is a nice young man. I don't think your mother and I will mind you going out with him.

Deirdre: (Kisses dad and goes to bed.) Well, at least something is going right.

Doreen: (She kisses dad.) Good night dad, don't let the bed bugs bite. (In the bedroom Doreen starts up again.) Deirdre's got a boyfriend, Deirdre's got a boyfriend.

Deirdre: (Yelling to Jack.) Dad, kill Doreen, she won't let me go to sleep. Let me alone, Doreen.

Jack: Girls don't have me come upstairs. Just be quiet and go to bed. Doreen, let Deirdre alone or I will let your mother know when she gets home.

Deirdre: Yeah, shut up Doreen. Otherwise you will get yours when mom gets home.

Doreen: OK I'll go to sleep, please don't tell mom.

Mary: How did your meeting with Lt. Castillo and his son go? Did you enjoy the food?

Jack: Everything went well. I didn't know both of the kids knew Caesar. The night was a big success for Deirdre. Caesar wants to start seeing her. He's a nice young man. I think you will like him.

Mary: He asked Deirdre out already?

Jack: Yes, he wants to take her out Friday night. I'm personally for it. We can invite him over so you get to know him.

Mary: OK I'll believe you. What I saw of him was impressive. He seems to have a touch of class like his father.

Jack: All of the Castillo children are well raised.

Mary: (After a good night of sleep, Deirdre is excited to see Caesar.) I hear somebody asked you out last night.

Deirdre: (With everybody looking at her, Deirdre gets a red face.) Come on mom, everybody is looking. (All of the girls get on Deirdre.)

Danielle: Doreen, did they hold hands and sit right next to each other?

Doreen: Yes, they sat close to each other and held hands. They shared popcorn; Caesar put his arm around her.

Deirdre: (Getting frustrated with tears.) Will everybody please shut up so I can eat?

Mary: All right, everybody needs to let Deirdre alone. It's all right honey; I'll talk to you later. Eat and get ready for school.

Deirdre: (Looks at Caesar with a big warm smile.) Hi Caesar, how are you?

Caesar: (With a big warm smile back.) I'm doing fine, sit with me. (The two hold hands and talk all the way to school.) Maybe it's time I met your mother.

Deirdre: Why don't you come home with me today? This way we can try to shore up plans for Friday night. I'm sure my mother will like you. Before we make plans, I will call her at lunch.

Deirdre: (At lunch with Caesar.) I will call my mother to make plans this evening.

Mary: Hello, who is it?

Deirdre: Hi mom, it's Deirdre. I was wondering if I could bring Caesar home for dinner tonight.

Mary: Although it's short notice, I would like to meet him. Make sure it's all right with his parents.

Deirdre: (Deirdre turns to Caesar.) Great news, my mother said you could come over as long as it's all right with your parents. Give your mother a call.

Caesar: We're half way there; I will give my mother a call right now.

Nadine: Hello, who is it?

Caesar: Hello mom, it's me. I was wondering if you would let me eat dinner over Deirdre's house this evening.

Nadine: That will be fine; I will pick you up around 7:30 this evening. Remember, you have homework tonight.

Caesar: Alright mom, I can't thank you enough. I will do my homework in study hall.

Nadine: That is fine, I want to pick you up and meet your new girlfriend and her mother.

Caesar: I will see you at 7:30 tonight. (While smiling at Deirdre.) Guess what, I can go. (The two share a kiss.)

Deirdre: I'm calling home so mom can set another place at the table.

Mary: Hello, who is it?

Deirdre: Mom, it's me again. If you don't mind, set another place at the table.

Mary: Great, I've wanted to get to know this guy. I will call dad and have him talk to Lt. Castillo about what Caesar likes to eat.

Deirdre: Mom, I could find out.

Mary: Please say nothing. I want to surprise him. I will see the two of you after school. (Mary calls Jack.) Hello honey, we have company tonight.

Jack: Who could that be?

Mary: Caesar is coming over for dinner. Could you ask your sidekick what Caesar really likes?

Jack: Carlos, what does Caesar like for dinner?

Lt. Castillo: He likes beef burritos and tacos. Make sure the beef is hot or have lots of hot sauce. He also likes chicken chimichangas.

Jack: It looks like Caesar likes beef burritos, tacos and chicken chimichangas. I was told to have the beef filling hot or to have a lot of hot sauce on hand. Is that enough to go on?

Mary: Yes, I will pick up the ingredients to make beef burritos and tacos. We will have steak and baked potatoes. Why not invite Carlos; we can have a small party.

Jack: Why not, I will see you around 6:00PM. Oh honey, do we have enough beer, wine, whiskey and tequila on hand. I can stop at the state store on the way home.

Mary: We could use some White Zinfandel and Tequila.

Jack: Consider it done. If the kids are hungry, I don't mind if you start without us.

Mary: I love you and will see you tonight.

Jack: I love you too. (Hangs up the phone and turns to Carlos.) Carlos, would you like to join us for dinner tonight?

Lt. Castillo: Why not, what is on the menu?

Jack: Beef burritos, tacos, steak and potatoes.

Lt. Castillo: Is there anything I can bring aside from myself?

Jack: Why not bring a bottle of tequila? We need to stop at the state store on the way home.

Lt. Castillo: (At the end of the work day.) Do you and Mary have a preference? If not, I like Jose Quervo and will get the one with the worm in it. Sounds like dinner will be a good one. I will follow you to the state store, then your house.

Deirdre: (Backing up to the end of the school day.) I can hardly wait to get home and introduce you to my mother. Please don't be nervous about the mom test. She is very easy to get along with and doesn't judge people.

Caesar: I'm still a little nervous, but a hot kiss may settle me down. (The two engage in a hot kiss and board the bus gazing into each others eyes.) I love you Deirdre. I want to kiss you again. (The two lock up in a lengthy French kiss.)

Bus Driver: (In his rear view mirror Bob sees the two putting on a kissing clinic.) Hey, the two of you need to come up for air.

Caesar: Bob, I'm in love. You should know I can't help myself.

Bus Driver: Try to get some control and come up for air. The two are putting on quite a show.

Caesar: We will try. (Bob turns his eyes to the road.) I love you Deirdre. (The two engage in another hot kiss.)

Bus Driver: Hey, I thought I told the two of you to stop.

Deirdre: (Embarrassed and red in the face.) We should wait until we get off the bus.

Caesar: I don't want to wait, but will.

Bus Driver: (As the bus stops Caesar and Deirdre begin to get off.) Caesar, this isn't your regular stop.

Caesar: I'm eating dinner over my girlfriends' house.

Bus Driver: Dating Deirdre now? She is a nice girl and a lot better than your last girlfriend. As far as impressing mom, don't worry. By the way, Mrs. Bordowski is very nice and a great cook. Have a good time.

Scene Nineteen: Forming New Friendships

Deirdre: (Arriving at home.) Mom, I'm home. I have a visitor.

Mary: Come in and don't be nervous. I'm Mary Bordowski, Deirdre's mother.

Caesar: I am Caesar; I'm pleased to meet you. (The two shake hands.)

Mary: Do the two of you want something to snack on or drink before your father and his guest arrive?

Caesar: You have a second guest?

Mary: Yes, your father is joining us for dinner.

Caesar: All right, smells like burritos.

Mary: That is only the start. Our first course will be chips with hot salsa and sopapillos. For desert we have Mexican Fried Ice Cream.

Caesar: How did you know the things I love?

Mary: I called your father at work.

Caesar: Did you want to eat some chips and salsa and sopapillos before everybody gets here?

Deirdre: I would love some. Let's go to the living room.

Mary: I'll bring everything in on folding tables. Just remember not to fill up.

Jack: Honey, I'm home.

Mary: Do you have our other guest?

Jack: Yes, we came home with big appetites and we need rest and relaxation.

Mary: Why don't the two of you come into the kitchen and get some snacks and beer. The appetizers will be chips with salsa and sopapillos. The main course will consist of several things: Beef burritos, tacos, steak and potatoes and refried beans. For dessert we have Mexican Fried Ice Cream.

Lt. Castillo: Dinner smells good. I will start up on some chips and salsa. By the way, did you use hot sauce in the burrito mix?

Mary: I used lots of hot sauce. Between the food and drink, your tongue should be between sting and burn.

Jack: Mary, before we go to the living room would you like a glass of wine and a shot?

Mary: Let's see what the two of you bought. White Zinfandel and Jose Quervo with a worm in it.

Lt. Castillo: Would you like the worm?

Mary: I used to love eating the worm in college.

Lt. Castillo: Let's pour the lady a glass of wine and a shot.

Mary: Let me get some limes and salt.

Lt. Castillo: Your wife is a pro at this.

Jack: In her day she could drink everybody under the table.

Mary: Let's eat a chip with salsa, and then make a toast.

Lt.Castillo: (After a chip.) Let's toast to great friends. (One toast goes down with lime and salt.)

Mary: I would like to raise another toast to two fine families and a bunch of great kids. (The second toast goes down.)

Jack: I have the third toast. To great food which I hope is ready soon. (The third toast goes down.)

Mary: You will soon have your choice of steak and baked potatoes or Mexican Food. I'm not floating badly so things will be done in five minutes. OK everybody, everything is ready and this is a come and get it night. Everybody can sit at the table or take a folding table into the living room and watch TV.

Jack: I'll start with one of everything.

Mary: Watch the alcohol with those burritos. You may want to try a little of the mix first.

Jack: Wow, I'm going to stick my head under the faucet with the cold water running. I will have one with dinner. I like heat among other things on my tongue.

Mary: As long as we don't get too drunk, we can have heat on the tongue now, and other things later. Trust that if we have a good time.

Jack: I won't get drunk. That will make sure we have a good time.

Lt. Castillo: Everything looks so good; I'll have one of everything. Caesar, I know what you want.

Caesar: Dad, since you're already here, maybe I should tell mom not to come.

Lt. Castillo: I will call your mother.

Nadine: Hello, who is it?

Lt. Castillo: It's me honey. I'm at the Bordowski household with Caesar eating dinner. I was calling to tell you that you don't have to pick him up.

Nadine: I still want to come over. I'm the only one who hasn't met Caesar's new girlfriend. I want to meet the whole Bordowski Family. Put me on the phone with Mrs. Bordowski.

Lt. Castillo: Mary, if you don't mind, my wife would like to speak to you.

Mary: I don't mind at all. I'll take the phone.

Nadine: Hi I'm Nadine, Caesar's mom. Would it be all right if my daughter and I join the party?

Mary: The more the merrier.

Nadine: Do you mind if I bring a few things over?

Mary: What are you thinking of?

Nadine: My husband and son usually eat more than once in an evening. I have tacos we could make. Do you have any burrito mix left?

Mary: Yes we do.

Nadine: We can have a great finish to this party with some tacos topped off with burrito mix. I will be over in about twenty minutes.

Mary: Great, I can hardly wait to meet you. (A little later Mary answers the door.) You must be Nadine, come in. Jack, girls, help Mrs. Castillo carry the food into the kitchen. Deirdre, you and I will go into the kitchen and help Mrs. Castillo prepare our second course. Jack and Carlos, we have beer, wine and shots of tequila in the kitchen. I want to know Nadine and make some toasts.

Nadine: It's so nice to meet you Mary, and especially you Deirdre. Could the two of you stay and gab a little while I get the second course ready?

Mary: (As drinks are poured.) I would like to propose my first toast. To making new friends. (The first toast goes down.)

Nadine: I would like to propose a second toast. To my son finding a decent girlfriend.

Lt. Castillo: (Laughing loud and hearty.) I'll second that. (The second toast goes down.)

Jack: We should have a third toast to a great get together. Let's watch how we pour this one. The person who wants the worm drinks from the bottle and must chew it before swallowing it.

Nadine: I haven't eaten a tequila worm in a long time.

Jack: Looks like Nadine gets the bottle.

Lt. Castillo: Honey, you're going to choke and puke.

Mary: Are you sure you want the worm?

Nadine: Yes, I sort of have to. Carlos is the best thing that ever happened to me. The only bad thing is that his impression of a woman is that we are soft.

Mary: I don't blame you. It could be these men will learn women are tough to. Let's get this toast together.

Lt. Castillo: I have to see this. My wife will puke for sure. (As the toast is made, Nadine starts to chew the worm and everyone is cheering her on.)

Mary: Let's go Nadine; let's show these big tough men what women are made of.

Jack: Let's get that thing down and hold it.

Lt. Castillo: I bet she throws up.

Jack: My money says she holds on for pride. Losing the worm will happen when we aren't looking.

Mary: Let's cheer the girl on; I've seen guys gag and puke doing this. Think of it this way, she isn't trying to show men up. All she is trying to show is that women can do the same things a man can do. Let's go Nadine, show that worm who's boss.

Lt. Castillo: I agree honey; don't let that worm kick your ass.

Jack: With seven women at home, I better be pro female. Let's hold on and swallow that worm.

Nadine: (Making faces as she swallows the worm and everybody cheers.) Where are the chips and salsa? I need food to hold this. (Nadine eats some chips and hot sauce.) Mary, if you don't mind my asking, is it all right to start the burrito mix.

Mary: Yes, let's get the second course under way. The burrito mix is in the fridge. Deirdre, if you don't mind, I will leave the two of you alone to get to know each other.

Deirdre: That will be fine mom.

Nadine: Could you help me unload these bags? There are many ingredients to a great taco. Tell me, did everybody serve themselves?

Deirdre: Yes, everybody served themselves.

Nadine: Good, it will take only a few minutes to get everything ready and we can join the party. Deirdre, could you set the backburner to medium and start the burrito mix.

Deirdre: I'll get right on it.

Nadine: After that, find me a skillet. If you don't know how, I'll show you how to brown ground beef. We need to set the front burner on high. (While sipping on wine.) We can work together to put the ingredients on the table. So Deirdre, how long have you known my son?

Deirdre: Since you moved into the area. Caesar and I have been in the same classes for months.

Nadine: I wish he asked you out rather than that thing he dated before.

Deirdre: Bonita Siaz is a though, nasty and dumb girl I think she's been held back twice. Whenever Caesar would talk to me, Bonita would get nasty. She threatened to beat me up if I looked at him.

Nadine: She called me a dumbass and told me to mind my own business in my own house. Caesar threw her out of the house and broke up with her right away. That was about two weeks ago. I just had to meet the nice girl my son said you were. Let's get our food and I will give you back to Caesar.

Deirdre: I've enjoyed our meeting. Don't worry about being disrespected; I'm a lot better than that. Let's get our food and join the party.

Nadine: (As the two women enter the living room.) All right everybody, the second course is ready.

Deirdre: (Sits down near Caesar.) Your parents seem so nice.

Caesar: They are the best and so are yours. After I get a snack we can get comfortable.

Doreen: (Whispering to Deirdre.) Did you kiss him? Did you meet his mother's approval?

Deirdre: (Snapping in a low tone.) Shut up and get lost. (Sitting close to Caesar.) You have to tell me what Bonita said to get you mad enough to throw her out.

Caesar: I will describe her in two words, shitty attitude. All my mother asked her was what got her interested in getting tattooed and pierced on her belly button and tongue. I will go into the story at my house. To tell you the truth, she told my mother to

68

shut up and mind my own business. I threw her out like a dog. As long as you respect my mother, we should get along.

Deirdre: Your mother is a fine woman. Don't worry about us getting along.

Nadine: Mary, I'm sorry I didn't get to speak to you much this evening. I wanted to get to know you and Deirdre. I must compliment you; she is so beautiful and well mannered.

Mary: Your son is also well raised. He is handsome and very intelligent.

Nadine: Can I have Deirdre over for dinner tomorrow before they go to the movies? I like to know the people he dates.

Mary: That will be fine. Has your son ever brought the wrong girl home?

Nadine: Yes, he brought this girl Bonita Siaz home. She was good looking but had a tough mouth. Caesar threw her out and we haven't seen her since. I didn't know they had class together until this evening.

Mary: Every once in awhile, my daughter said Bonita threatened her in private for talking to and smiling at him.

Nadine: I'm very sorry. I believe she is emotionally disturbed. She has an older sister named Sadie. She is in a juvenile detention center for fighting and generally hating and hurting people.

Mary: Jack was instrumental in putting her away. Sadie beat my daughter Dallas up. She was on medication for depression. Apparently part of her probation was to stay on the medication. Apparently she skipped her medication when she wanted and beat four people up before she beat our daughter Dallas up. In an effort to work with Sadie, the school did nothing to either student. All the administration said was that Sadie forgot her medication.

Nadine: I wonder if Bonita and Sadie have the same disorder. I also didn't know that taking medication could be part of probation.

Mary: That was to control the violence. What little I know of Caesar, he won't let Bonita start with Deirdre.

Nadine: I'm certain he wouldn't. You should see the way Caesar threw her out of the house and our lives. Deirdre will be safe with Caesar by her side.

Mary: Is there a way we can exchange telephone numbers so we can have a cup of coffee or go shopping together? I would also like you to meet my sidekick Laura Davidson. Who knows what kind of trouble we can get into?

Nadine: I would like to meet her. Bill is our doctor. He's not only a great doctor; he is very handsome and intelligent.

Mary: I'll say that. He makes everything from a suit to biker's clothing look good. Laura is so lucky, she got a great looking guy who has a good attitude and doesn't fool around.

Nadine: I would like to join the two of you out. Oh my goodness, it's ten o'clock. Carlos, we have to go.

Deirdre: Caesar, it's been such a great night. I will see you tomorrow for dinner. (The two sneak a kiss before the Castillos leave.)

Nadine: (Both women exchange numbers before leaving.) I will be in contact. (In the car.) This time you picked a very nice girl. We will see her for dinner tomorrow. Before you make plans for Deirdre, she will be going shopping with me. I want some of her time.

Caesar: When will I see her?

Nadine: When I am finished getting to know her. You will see plenty of Deirdre tomorrow. You should go to bed when we get home, it's getting late. I take it you did your homework in study hall today. Oh by the way, I like this girl. You can see her anytime you want.

Mary: (Sending the kids to bed.) OK girls, everybody upstairs. Jack, I had a great time. I really like Caesar. As far as I'm concerned, he can see Deirdre anytime. I like the whole Castillo Family. Nadine seems nice and fun loving. I hope to be in contact soon.

Jack: The two of you seemed to have a good time. Get to know her better.

Mary: I plan to, but now it's time to get close and know you better.

Jack: (Mary begins to kiss Jack on the love seat in the den area.) Love is always fun and interesting with you.

Mary: One can't confine love to the bedroom only. (The two make love for an hour in the den and start over in the bedroom.)

Deirdre: (On the bus.) Hey there, handsome.

Caesar: Hi, beautiful, grab a seat. I'm already waiting for the school day to end. I think my mother has plans to take you shopping for dinner.

Deirdre: I will need some time with her. I don't mind because I like your mom. We will probably shop, cook and set the table. You won't have to worry about me mouthing off like your other girlfriend.

Deirdre: I will have plenty of time for you. Did you finish your homework yesterday?

Caesar: I did it in study hall. What you do about yours?

Deirdre: I suffered through it last night. I had dreams of us together. Being around you makes me feel so good. I can hardly wait for the school day to end. (Looking deep into Caesar's eyes.) I love you. (The two share a quick soft kiss.)

Caesar: I love you. (As the bus stops at school.) I will see you at class. I don't like the way Bonita looks at you. I need to be alone because I have an old score to settle and I may say some things that aren't nice.

Deirdre: Try not to be too mean. This could come my way.

Bonita: (Getting off the bus.) What does that bitch have that I don't?

Caesar: She has a great personality and knows how to get along with people. What I mean to say is she is a decent person and you aren't.

Bonita: I bet you haven't got past kissing with her. Is she still a virgin? I know you'll be back.

Caesar: The only part of me that misses you is my midsection. That isn't enough to come back. I don't miss the rest of you.

Bonita: All I want to do is kick that bitch's ass.

Caesar: If you look at her wrong, I'll kick your ass.

Bonita: I thought you were a gentleman.

Caesar: Try acting like a lady and I might treat you like one. I don't want you bothering Deirdre and me.

Bonita: You can have your Virgin Mary. I know you'll come running back.

Caesar: I'll never come back, goodbye and good luck.

Deirdre: (Back in class.) What did you tell her?

Caesar: I told Bonita to stop watching us and disappear.

Deirdre: I'm glad you told her to disappear, but I hope you weren't too mean.

Caesar: I was authoritative but not too mean. That message makes tonight even better. It means I want only you. Let's enjoy our time together and forget Bonita.

Bonita: (At the end of the school day.) Hey bitch, what are you doing?

Deirdre: Saving my boyfriend a seat.

Bonita: That will be for a short time only.

Caesar: I told you straight, we are through.

Bonita: That's what you think. I'm going to kick your girlfriend's ass one of these days.

Caesar: Turn around and shut up or I'll kick your ass. (Bonita turns around with a sneer.)

Scene Twenty: Deirdre Passes the Mom Test

Deirdre: She doesn't get off at your stop does she?

Caesar: No we get off before her. Let's enjoy our evening. (The lovebirds get off the bus.) I love you and won't let anything happen to you. Bonita will pay for this. (The two kiss so Bonita can see it. Disgusted, Bonita gives them the finger as the bus drives off.) Welcome to my neck of the woods. Let's go to my house.

Deirdre: Wow, your house is bigger than our house. How many brothers and sisters do you have?

Caesar: I only have one sister. Her name is Denise, she was over last night.

Deirdre: Please remember, I spent my night between you and your mother. Please make sure you introduce me. Your sister can tell me all the dirt on you.

Caesar: That's just what I need. (As they enter the house.) Hi mom, we're here.

Nadine: Why don't both of you come into the kitchen? Deirdre, would you like to come on a short shopping trip with me? I need to surprise some people for dinner.

Deirdre: Yes, where are we going?

Nadine: We are getting something to eat. Even though I have everything to make tacos and burritos, I am having seafood tonight. We will buy some of your favorites, blue claw crabs and flounder. This trip won't take long. Caesar, stay here with your father and sister.

Deirdre: How did you know I like seafood?

Nadine: A little birdie told me.

Deirdre: Probably my mother. Let's get going. By the way, where are you going?

Nadine: We are going to Under the Pier. We will get a dozen Blue Claw Crabs.

Deirdre: Do you spice your crabs?

Nadine: We will boil in two pots. My husband doesn't like too much spice on his seafood. The flounder won't take long to broil. I have all the spice you like and some lemons. Let's get going. (Passing the rose garden.) Do you put flowers in your hair? If so we will pose as two taken women.

Deirdre: Sounds good, I will have to show my mother where this place is. She always goes to the supermarket. (While picking out crabs.) Wow this place has it all, clams, muscles, fish lobsters and crabs. (Getting back from the trip the girls pass the roses.) Let's put some roses in our hair.

Nadine: Do you like white or red?

Deirdre: What about these yellow roses?

Nadine: We can't wear yellow that color is for jealousy.

Deirdre: I will take red.

Nadine: I will take white. Put it in your right side. That means we are taken.

Lt. Castillo: How long until dinner is done?

Nadine: About forty-five minutes to an hour.

Lt. Castillo: I see you are taken tonight. Tell me about this man.

Nadine: He is five foot ten, medium build, brown hair, brown skin, and handsome. I have been with him for fifteen years. He is the man for me.

Lt. Castillo: Would you be free for a dinner date?

Nadine: I don't know. Would it be right for my man?

Lt. Castillo: (Laughing pretty hard.) OK my dear, I can see this will be a great dinner.

Caesar: What are you doing in the kitchen?

Deirdre: Getting the pot ready to boil if you step out of line. Come in and let's boil some crabs up. We have two pots, one with spice and one without.

Caesar: I want two without spice; I take care of it at the table.

Deirdre: Will you kiss me after dinner? I like a lot of spice.

Caesar: (After a soft kiss.) I couldn't imagine a day without kissing you. (While at the table.) Dad, do you have chores I could do for money?

Lt. Castillo: Yes, but those things will be done at a different time. What will you be doing and how much will you need?

Caesar: I want to see a movie with Deirdre on Friday.

Lt. Castillo: Don't stay all night. Boxing begins on Saturday. We will be working out steadily for four weeks before our first competition. Your mother, sister and I are traveling to see your Aunt Kathy. We will be home at 11:00 at night and take Deirdre home.

Caesar: Sounds good dad, can I have the money tomorrow?

Lt. Castillo: Yes, but remember, that money is for future chores. On Friday, we will see one of the movies at Oxford Valley Mall. We will take the bus.

Nadine: Carlos, Mary talked me into joining the PTA.

Carlos: Does this mean we will see better grades out of Denise?

Denise: Dad!!! I pass all of my subjects with a C or above. What do you want out of me?

Lt. Castillo: To do better in school.

Nadine: I want you to start helping out around the house a bit more. You should at least be helping me with cooking and cleaning. You will have to know about these things when you get married.

Denise: Mom and dad, I may get interested in these things later. For now at the age of eleven, girls just want to have fun so let me alone. In the future, I will make sure I don't have to learn these things because I will marry a rich man. We will have a maid and eat out all of the time.

Deirdre: (Laughing pretty hard.) You have a great plan. I think I will do the same. That will be a great and easy life.

Caesar: Deirdre, you will force me to be a professional boxer to keep you around.

Deirdre: You don't have to be a millionaire to keep me. I wouldn't know one if I saw one. Where would you start to look?

Denise: (Looking at dad.) Anywhere but the police force.

Lt. Castillo: What is wrong with what I do?

Denise: You put your life on the line and don't get rich. When I get old enough I will go to all of the expensive clubs and rock concerts. I might marry a rock star.

Deirdre: You and I need to talk so I can get the dirt on Caesar.

Denise: We need to talk at school without Caesar around.

Caesar: (A nasty tone.) Denise, I swear if you do that I'll knock you out.

Nadine: (An irritable tone.) Caesar, you won't touch anyone. Do you know what movie you are going to see?

Caesar: There are eight to choose from, it will be an on the spot decision.

Lt. Castillo: Sounds good to me.

Caesar: (Directly after dinner.) Mom, do I get to see some of my girlfriend now? I want to see some of the James Bond movie You Only Live Twice. (While on the couch.) You asked me if I would kiss you. I need to taste some of the spices on your tongue.

Deirdre: (The two engage in a hot French kiss.) I think I will eat my crabs with the spices you use. (The two curl up, kiss and see the movie.)

Lt. Castillo: Caesar and Deirdre, it's time to go home, both of you have homework. You can do that tonight or do it early tomorrow morning.

Scene Twenty: Preparation for a Big Date.

Deirdre: (The second she gets home Deirdre finds Dallas.) Can I speak to you in private?

Dallas: Sure, so what is on your mind?

Deirdre: I have a hot date coming up. Caesar has already made love and I haven't looked at or touched a guy beneath the clothes. I need to make sure he doesn't return to his old girlfriend or start looking for another. Can you give me some tips on what to do?

Dallas: I will only tell you about two things, touching and oral sex. The rest you have to talk to mom about. The million dollar question before I begin is: Do you love him?

Deirdre: With all of my heart. Why is that important?

Dallas: Because that guy will attach to you and you could get the reputation of a slut. If are you are sure Caesar is yours, start kissing him hot. The things I will show and tell you should be done by couples in love because guys attach to sex. The first thing you must do is look and smell your best. Make sure you begin with kissing, soft touch and holding. (Dallas talks about how to touch and orally handle Caesar.)

Deirdre: Can you talk to me about going all the way?

Dallas: No, you're too young and have to go to mom.

Deirdre: Can you show me how to touch and have oral sex?

Scene Twenty-One: Caught in the Act.

Dallas: That much I can do. I'll get a few bananas. Deirdre, don't do anything until you've observed me. (Dallas gets a firm grip and runs her hand up and down the banana. Mary watches Deirdre do the same thing. With both girls giggling up a storm. Mary watches Dallas peel the banana, lick the end awhile, and stick it deep down her throat. As Dallas repeats the action, Mary enters the living room.)

Mary (In a nasty tone.) Dallas, (Dallas bites the banana in half and begins choking and chewing on it.) I see you have a mouthful. I will speak to the two of you in the morning. (Sticking her tongue in her cheek.) Dallas and Deirdre, is there something we need to talk about. I may know something about the subject.

Dallas: (While choking and chewing on the banana.) No mom, everything is fine.

Mary: (In a sharp tone.) Dallas, you and I will have a serious talk tomorrow. I know what you were showing Deirdre and at only the age of thirteen! (Now calmly toward Deirdre.) Deirdre, since you are getting serious with someone, there are some things you must know.

Deirdre: Can't it wait until tomorrow?

Mary: Yes, both of you go to bed. (The following morning.) Dallas and Deirdre, I need to speak to both of you. (In a nasty tone.) Dallas, I want you in the kitchen now.

Dallas: (In the living room with Deirdre.) Mom is going to read me the riot act. Did you learn anything?

Deirdre: I learned a lot and plan on putting it into practice tomorrow night. I may practice a pulling session after school today.

Dallas: Mom is going to tell you not to do these things.

Deirdre: It will be fine if mom doesn't want me having sex of any kind. She simply never has to know.

Mary: Dallas, this will be the first and last time I speak to you about showing and telling the other girls about sexual favors. Don't let me catch you doing that again.

Dallas: I'm sorry mom, can I leave? Are you going to punish me?

Mary: I should but won't. Don't let it happen again. (In a decent tone of voice.) Deirdre, please come to the kitchen. Deirdre, I know what Dallas was showing you and you're too young to touch boys their in private places. Although you can't get pregnant from oral sex, it leads to other things.

Deirdre: Did Dallas do everything right?

Mary: Unfortunately, all too well.

Deirdre: How old were you when you first touched a boy's body?

Mary: I was only fifteen. At first I felt scared but he was my first love. I'm not going into details, but it was the best and worst experience of my life.

Deirdre: What made it the best?

Mary: I chose to make love to a man I loved. Love with soft touching is the best in my opinion.

Deirdre: What made it the worst?

Mary: I knew I was doing something I shouldn't have done. We will talk more, but I have to get breakfast for eight people. I also need to get six girls off to school.

Deirdre: Mom, can I stay at school late? I need to use the library for some research on my science project. I will take the late activity bus home.

Mary: Yes, please be home by 6:00PM.

Scene Twenty-Two: Love Starts to Blossom.

Deirdre: (Before school on the bus.) Honey, can we walk down to Dairy Queen after school and get some ice cream? I want to spend some time with you.

Caesar: I will call my mother and see if I can. (Caesar gets yes as an answer.) Good news, beautiful; we have a date after school.

Deirdre: (The two kiss.) I can hardly wait for the end of the day. (As the school day ends.) Let's walk down to the Dairy Queen. Then I want to take a walk in the woods with you.

Caesar: Where do you want to go?

Deirdre: Down to the creek. I want to set romantic history. I want to teach you the touching lessons of love.

Caesar: What will you teach me?

Deirdre: Have you ever heard of blooping or taste testing ice cream from a hot French kiss. (In a soft voice.) I want to hold you in a private place in the woods. I want to touch you so badly it hurts. I love you so much.

Caesar: I love what I hear. I have some money, let's get an ice cream and go to a private place in the woods. There is a nice place along the creek with big rocks to sit on. We will find a lot of privacy there.

Deirdre: I'm warning you, we can't go all the way.

Caesar: I don't need that now. I can wait for you.

Deirdre: (After buying some ice cream.) Let's taste each others ice cream with some deep hot kissing. (The two lick each others ice cream and engage in a deep hot kiss. Both hearts are gently pounding.) Close your eyes. I need to walk you to the creek and throw a rock in the water. When the rock hits the water we kiss.

Caesar: Let me be a gentleman. Close your eyes. Don't worry; I would never let you fall. Sit down slowly and don't open your eyes. (Deirdre sits on a rock with Caesar and he throws a rock in the water. The two engage in a long deep kiss.)

Deirdre: (In a soft voice.) I want to touch you so bad. I also want you to touch me. (Both look around and loosen their clothes.) This is only for you Caesar. (After the two finish loving each other, Deirdre hears people approaching; the two straighten up their clothing and leave.) It's time to go home. Let's head back to the bus honey. I love you and want a repeat performance tomorrow night. I want to go further but not all the way. (As the bus let's Deirdre off.) I really don't want to leave you but I promised to be home for dinner. I can hardly wait for tomorrow night.

Caesar: I will tell my parents we will stop for ice cream; this guarantees they will be gone when we get to my house.

Mary: (As Deirdre walks in.) Sit down; we're ready to eat dinner if you have room.

Dallas: (Sticks her tongue in her cheek with a smile.) Did you eat ice cream?

Danielle: Tell me about Romeo.

Daisy: Did he kiss you or at least hold your hand?

Doreen: Are you going to marry him?

Deirdre: (Quietly in a low tone.) We didn't do what you think. We ate ice cream, blooped, talked and held each other. (Deirdre runs her hand up and down a spoon with full grip.)

Doreen: Deirdre's got a boyfriend, Deirdre's got a boyfriend.

Deirdre: (Loud and direct.) Shut up Doreen! Will everybody please let me eat?

Mary: We will start with salad and move to the main course. I also have a vegetable plate with dressing.

Dallas: I will start with carrots and celery sticks. (Starts licking the end of the carrot with her tongue and the girls laugh.)

Deirdre: (Grabs a big carrot and runs her hand up and down.) That is the furthest I went with him. I will try the rest tomorrow.

Mary: Dallas, I need to speak with you in the kitchen. You know what I saw. I don't appreciate you showing the girls oral sex and how to touch a man. I know you started very early, but that doesn't mean you speak of it to a thirteen year old. If she asks you about sleeping with a man you will direct her to me. If you hold to that promise I won't punish you for what you did.

Dallas: OK mom, I don't want to get into a fight. I'm sorry about what I showed her.

Mary: Very well, your father will be home in a few minutes. We can start to eat right now. Just remember what I told you and we will remain at peace. (Out at the table.) Deirdre, make sure you don't go anywhere after dinner. You aren't in trouble but we have to talk. Please enjoy dinner without gripping carrots and spoons with your entire hand.

Deirdre: OK mom, I'm sorry.

Doreen: Can we hear more about Caesar?

Deirdre: Doreen, let me eat.

Mary: All of you please let Deirdre eat.

Scene Twenty-Three: Great News at Dinner

Jack: (Walks in the front door.) Sorry I'm late. I got some great news. Chief Green will retire in the next year or two and I am up for chief. He spoke to me about the details.

Mary: Honey that is fabulous. Does he know when?

Jack: Not at this time. Chief Green said he would keep me posted. I got some White Zinfandel to toast the news. Everybody eat while I pour the wine. Let me propose a toast to a better life.

Mary: (The two have a toast.) We will talk later, dinner can't wait.

Dallas: Dad, does this mean more money and that you will buy me a new car?

Jack: It does mean more money. A new car still won't be in the budget.

Doreen: Does this mean you will be telling everybody what to do?

Jack: Yes, but Chief of Police means more than getting your way.

Doreen: I'm going to tell everybody at school.

Jack: Please say nothing until I get the job. The promotion is at least a year away. If anything should go wrong, minds could change. By the way Deirdre, what movie are you and Caesar going to see tomorrow?

Deirdre: We haven't decided, with several theatres playing it will be an on the spot decision.

Mary: Will you be home for dinner?

Deirdre: No, I'm going straight to the Castillo's house, then to the movies.

Darlene: Let us know what movie you see and how much of it you see.

Daisy: Tell us if you make a movie.

Danielle: Let us know the blow by blow details.

Mary: (A little emphatic.) Girls, that will be enough.

Jack: Deirdre, don't keep Caesar up to all hours in the night. He starts boxing workouts Saturday.

Doreen: Dad, I can't wait to get started. You were right, Virginia is a great fighter.

Scene Twenty-Four: Round Two Mother Versus Daughter over Boxing.

Mary: Doreen, boxing isn't for girls.

Doreen: Oh yeah, my hero is Sandra O'Shea and she is a boxer.

Mary: Most women don't choose careers that involve their fists. Is she a lady? Jack, do you see what you've done to our daughter watching and teaching her to fight.

Doreen: Mom, Sandra's public appearance is great. She raises money for charities. She also speaks out on issues of the times and dedications. Sandra is a boxer and a modern day credit to her gender. She is someone to be proud of. Her father is a doctor who boxed. Her training started with him. The way you love children, how can't you call her a female role model. Most of the charities she raises money for are for children.

Mary: I still feel you need to pick a role model who doesn't break faces and ribs. I really don't want you boxing or wrestling, these aren't things ladies do.

Doreen: Mom, the definition of a lady has changed since you were young. Since the woman's lib movement in the early seventies, a woman can be what she wants.

Mary: Honey, you're only eleven years old. This is too early to call yourself a woman.

Doreen: Sorry mom, a girl's got to do what a girl's got to do. Saturday morning I will report to boxing practice with dad.

Mary: (With a sharp look at Jack.) Jack, after dinner I need a short word with you.

Jack: (With a long face.) Certainly dear, what about when you're doing the dishes?

Mary: That will be fine. (With a cross tone in the kitchen.) I'll be brief with you. I don't like the fact Doreen will be boxing. It is a heavy contact sport and the teaching of violence. The only reason I'm not fighting this hard is that Doreen will side with you and hold this against me. Boxing will not come between my daughter and me. I warn you that if she brings it home and uses violence to settle matters, boxing will come between you and me. I'm trying to raise a house of six perfect ladies. I thought Dallas would be my only challenge. Now I'll have two to watch over. Doreen will turn out a perfect lady and guess who will make sure of it.

Jack: Honey, I want her to be a lady too. I will make sure as will Virginia Lopez that she won't use it for more than competition and self defense.

Mary: My final words are here. I can't wait until this blows up in your face. I'm finished with this conversation. (Mary figures she has been hard on Jack. She finishes the dishes, takes a bath and wants to make up and celebrate the good news. Mary puts her sexiest night gown on and has a plan for makeup and celebration sex.) Girls, it's time to go to bed. Jack, I'll join you in the den in a few minutes. I promise it won't be bad. (Mary comes into the den removing her robe to show a see through night gown with no bra and sexy underwear.) I propose a toast to you being promoted and being a great and understanding husband. (The two bite strawberries and sip champagne.)

Jack: I propose a toast to the greatest wife in the world. (The two toast and begin a hot kiss.)

Mary: (Slowly removing her gown and softly speaking in Jack's ear.) Touch me all over honey; I want to love you so bad. (Jack begins fondling Mary's left breast while placing two fingers in her warm wet tunnel of love. Mary moans loudly.) AHHH keep them in there. Suck on my nipples.

Danielle: (Up in the bedroom.) Mom and dad at it again.

Dallas: Yeah, mom gets pretty loud. Dad must give it right. At least I've learned to sleep through it.

Jack: (Whispering in Mary's ear.) Let me go down on you honey.

Mary: (Mary lies back on the couch as Jack starts licking Mary's clitoris she begins to orgasm.) AHHH!!! AHHH!!! Keep going. I'm cumming, keep going. I'm cumming, don't stop. Let's take this to the floor honey. (The two go to the floor. Mary takes Jack's throbbing flesh into her mouth.)

Jack: (Mary begins bobbing her head slowly and taking him deep into her mouth.) Honey, it feels so good. Keep going, it feels so good. (After awhile Jack cums in her mouth. With a sip of champagne Mary swallows his seed.)

Mary: (In a low voice.) That thing is harder than hell and we can't have that. Lay back and enjoy honey. (Mary mounts Jack's throbbing flesh from the top and drives Jack nuts with a slow deep grinding motion.)

Jack: Honey, you're so good to me I can't believe it. Shake your hips a little faster; I'm going to cum. (After his second orgasm.) Let me take the top.

Mary: (In a low voice Mary Directs Jack.) Stroke me slow and deep, hold me tight honey. I'm already cumming, I love you so much Jack. (In a loud moan.) Keep going, keep going, AHHH! AHHH! I'm cumming so hard. (As Jack tightens his grip on Mary, she wraps her arms and legs tightly around him with her body quivering, heavy breathing and moaning. After thirty minutes of a tightly wrapped love session, Jack cums deep inside of Mary.) This time I got you. It's finally starting to dwindle. I love you Jack.

Jack: I love you too. Let's turn in for the evening. Let's curl up tight for the night.

Mary: (In the morning with a smile.) It's time for breakfast girls.

Jack: Deirdre, don't keep Caesar up to all hours of the night. We know the Castillos won't have you home until 11:30 PM. Please remember boxing workouts begin tomorrow morning.

Deirdre: OK dad, I won't send him there worn out.

Danielle: Tell us how much of the movie you see.

Darlene: Tell us what movie you see, that if you see enough and can remember.

Mary: OK if you're done eating, let's get moving for the buses.

Caesar: (Saving Deirdre a seat.) Hello beautiful, sit next to me. (He lightly strokes her leg.) I love you.

Deirdre: (Removes his hand from her leg.) I love you too honey, but we are in public. At least wait for ice cream after school.

Caesar: I can hardly wait for the day to end.

Deirdre: Remember; let's stop for ice cream before going to your house. (End of the school day.) Give me a kiss hot stuff and we can go get some ice cream.

Scene Twenty-Five: The big Date

Caesar: Your wish is my command. (The two kiss and walk to the Dairy Queen.) What will you have my dear.

Deirdre: A chocolate and vanilla swirl.

Caesar: I will have a chocolate cone. Do we bloop again?

Deirdre: No, but I want to walk to the creek and sit for awhile.

Caesar: I don't blame you for wanting to see everything around you.

Deirdre: (As they sit by the creek.) Let's take our time getting back to your place. I want to start the party by the creek. Let's taste each others ice cream, get close, kiss and touch all over. Let's loosen up these clothes' I really want to get close. (While kissing and touching each other all over: Deirdre begins to moan, with her senses out of control, Deirdre drops her ice cream.)

Caesar: I love you so much. Honey, you dropped your ice cream, do you want another one?

Deirdre: I'm not hungry for ice cream. I'm only hungry for love. Let's get on the bus and go to your house. I want to love you without our clothes on.

Deirdre: (As the two get to the Castillo Household, they climb under a blanket on the couch and remove their clothes. Both experience tremendous pleasure as they kiss and touch all over. Deirdre cleans with her hanky and forgets it under the couch. The two shower, go to get a bite to eat, and see the rerun of Thunderball.)

Caesar: Let's catch the bus to the Oxford Valley Mall. We can get a bite to eat at Friendlys and go to the movies.

Deirdre: Can we go to the food court first? Some of our friends may be there. After we get to the movie we can head to the back corner and make out like the horny teenagers we are.

Caesar: Now you're talking. (The two go to the food court and run into two friends, Anna and Paul who are going to see a movie.) Anna what movie are you going to see?

Anna: We are undecided. It really doesn't matter when you don't see much of it. Caesar and Deirdre, did you hear of the beer party over Eddie Driscoll's House tomorrow?

Caesar: Yes, I don't know if I can make it. Boxing starts tomorrow. Why don't you see the Bond Movie with us? Despite you won't see much of the movie, what you see will be good. It will be constant action.

Anna: Sounds good to me. I'm a Bond Fan anyway.

Paul. Let's see Thunderball.

Deirdre: Hey hot stuff; make sure you are looking at me instead of those hot Bond Girls.

Caesar: I plan on seeing so much of you; I couldn't tell you what a Bond Girl looks like. I consider you My Bond Girl.

Deirdre: (In a soft voice.) I love you Caesar. Let's find a quiet corner in the back of the theatre. I want to curl up to my star. (After two hours of making out at the movies the couple goes back to the Castillo Household.)

Caesar: We need to clean up all clues of what we were doing. After that we have a few hours before my parents get home. (The two miss the hanky under the couch. They think all of the clues are cleaned up and curl up on the couch.)

Nadine: (As the Castillo's get home.) How are the two love birds doing?

Caesar: We are fine mom. We saw an old James Bond movie we never saw before. Thunderball was great.

Lt. Castillo: (Quietly hands Deirdre a hanky he found on the floor.) Would this be yours?

Deirdre: Yes, thank you Lt. Castillo.

Caesar: Oh yeah, the sneeze you had from your allergies.

Deirdre: The ragweed is terrible at this time of year.

Lt. Castillo: Deirdre, it's getting late and time to get you home. Caesar, come with us. (As they get Deirdre home.) See the young lady in.

Caesar: That was close. Do you think they know?

Deirdre: I hope not. I love you Caesar. (The two kiss goodnight.)

Caesar: I love you too.

Lt. Castillo: I need you to level with me. The two of you either didn't see a movie or went to an early show and came back. I promise you no punishment for the truth. Were you sleeping with her? I already know you went all the way with Bonita. That hanky wasn't cemented together with snot. You're quite lucky I found it instead of your mother.

Caesar: We didn't go all the way. It was oral sex and touching. I know we will go all the way, but I don't know when.

Lt. Castillo: I want you to start using condoms. If she gets pregnant, both childhoods disappear whether she has the baby or not. I don't want to see that happen to either of you.

Caesar: I will look into them but I'm not old enough to buy them.

Lt. Castillo: I will handle that. Let's get some sleep, boxing workouts begin tomorrow. Get a good night sleep. Since we spoke, I know I will. I will say nothing to your mother.

Scene Twenty-Six: Official Workouts Begin

Dallas: (Answers the phone.) Hello, who is it?

Caesar: Hello, it's Caesar Castillo. I was wondering if Deirdre was awake.

Dallas: Hold on Romeo, I mean Caesar. Deirdre, Romeo is on the phone and he can't live without you.

Deirdre: All right Dallas, give me the phone.

Caesar: I was wondering if you could come up to the gym at Middletown Police Dept. where I am working out. I really want to see you.

Deirdre: (With a smart-alecky tone.) What is in it for me?

Caesar: (With a tone of the same.) You get to see your favorite guy in shorts and a tee shirt.

Deirdre: I would rather see you with no clothes on at all.

Caesar: You saw that most of last night. I'm in public now.

Deirdre: I was just kidding, I will ask Dallas for a ride when we hang up. I will be there in about twenty minutes.

Caesar: Great, I can hardly wait to see you. I love you honey.

Deirdre: I love you and will see you later. Dallas, can you give me a ride to the gym.

Dallas: Yes, I need to meet hot stuff. I will take you around 10:30. I also have to ask dad if I can go to a concert with Eddie Driscoll.

Deirdre: Is that the family on Upland Drive with all the parties and loud music?

Dallas: Yes, mom and dad got into a fight over dad letting me go to a party there.

Doreen: (On the way to the gym.) Dad, I'm so excited. I hope I'm not one of a few that decide to stick with this.

Jack: If we're lucky, more than last week will show up.

Doreen: I can hardly wait to start working out with Virginia. She is such a good instructor. If I can handle it, I want to box and wrestle.

Jack: Sgt. Lopez is quite a woman. She is fighting crime on the street by day, professionally boxes by night as well as wrestling and competing in judo for team USA and their traveling team; she can teach you quite a bit.

Doreen: Wow, she is a walking arsenal. I can't wait to start training.

Jack: Look at how good the turnout is. I think we have five or six more girls here. It could be that having a real professional boxer and cop helped the cause.

Doreen: There must be fifteen to twenty girls there. Dad, the woman carrying the bag, is that Virginia.

Jack: That would be her. Virginia always carries that neat as a pin with sunglasses look.

Doreen: (After they park.) Dad, I will see you in a few hours.

Jack: You will see me in a few seconds because I run the whole program. I will speak to everybody before we get started. Now join the rest of the girls. (Jack grabs a microphone in the gym.) Good morning everybody, I'm Lt. Bordowski. I'm in charge of the PAL League Boxing and Wrestling Teams. For the girls, SGT Virginia Lopez is in charge of your workouts and will be in your corner when competing in the ring. I will periodically be around.

Jack: For the guys, Lt. Castillo and I will be in charge of your training and in your corner when competing. Should you see or hear from Sgt. Lopez, make sure you listen up and respect her. All girls follow Sgt. Lopez to the lower gym. Guys, stay where you are so we can divide you up into a few groups. (With a show of hands, Jack and Carlos find out how many boxers and wrestlers are on hand. Jack sees that there are enough for a starting lineup of fighters and backups. There will be enough to have boxing matches every week and to have people rotated. The next show of hands was for people who wanted to learn the basics but not go competitive.) For those who came down to learn to defend themselves only, you will be working out with the boxers but will not have to fight or spar in the ring unless you feel ready for contact.

Sgt. Lopez: OK girls, I'm Virginia Lopez. I will be your instructor and coach. The first thing I need is a show of hands. I need the girls who don't want to compete to raise their hands. (Not one girl raised their hand. Virginia smiles and comments.) This is great, I have all competitive girls. In these classes we will learn three forms of competition: boxing, wrestling and judo. To my right are two police Sargeants out of the Philadelphia Police Force. Sgt. Lori Foley and Sgt. Terri Foster. They will assist in training all of you. One of the three of us will be in the corner with you in the boxing and wrestling ring. Despite not yet big, the PAL League has judo competitions, give me a show of hands for girls who want to compete in judo. (Only one girl raises her hand.) This is great, I wasn't sure if anyone would be interested. Don't be worried, most of the precincts don't have anyone who does this. There are only twenty-two girls enrolled in Bucks County, but I can find you at least a match every other week that counts for record, and if you get good enough and want a match a week, you can come to the judo club with me and have a match per week. What is your name?

Janet: I'm Janet Houser, are you sure you can have a team with only one person?

Sgt. Lopez: Yes, because there aren't enough girls signed up to form a team in Bucks County. The only difference is that only the top ten are recognized because of a lack of girls and that all competitions will be held on Wednesday Nights at 7:30PM at the Fairless Gym so everybody has to travel. You and I will work out with the wrestlers because the mats will be down. Now I have to get a show of hands for the girls who want to box and wrestle. I see I have a good amount of boxers but I'm a little short on wrestlers. I need two or three backup girls I can call if someone is sick or can't make weight.

Doreen: Are we allowed to participate in more than one form of competition? I like wrestling too.

Sgt. Lopez: Yes, because the competitions are held on different days. (Both Denise and Doreen raise there hands.) Now I have good competitive numbers on all events. I will need all backups to watch their weight. The instructors will meet with the wrestlers at the gym at 10:00AM on Saturday and 3:30PM for an hour during the week. Boxers we will meet with you on Saturday at 11:00AM and weeknights at 4:30PM for an hour. The only exception will be today since all of the instructors are here. Everybody has open use of the gym to work out on Sunday which I suggest with only four weeks to our first competition. Wrestlers please go with Sgt. Foster to the mats, I will be over there periodically to assist with instruction, and all boxers to the heavy bags please. I will be with Sgt. Foley for a little while. We will show you how to move your feet and get into a good stance. Make sure that your chin is tucked in at all times because taking a hard punch in that area or the jaw line can be very painful and good for a knockout. Sgt. Foley, if you would move the bag for me for a minute I can demonstrate footwork. Girls, as you can see you shouldn't stand flatfooted, move in and out backward and foreword with your opponent and never give that person a stationary target to hit. (After demonstrating on the bag.) Remember, the best punches are not always the hardest. A good punch is in how good you hit your opponent. Sgt. Foley, let's divide the class in half so we can have one girl holding the bag while another punches. We can talk about who and what we have and have some of the better girls help those who need help. I do need to get with Sgt. Foster in about fifteen to twenty minutes to help out over there. I see we have six girls who really know what they are doing. Sgt. Foley, I need to rob two of our better boxers so they can get some wrestling instruction and things will be on different time schedules starting Monday. I will see you Monday unless you need to speak after training. I have to tend to the wrestlers and my judo student for at least a half hour. (Virginia moves on with the wrestlers.) Good work Sgt. Foster, it looks like you have had these girls paired up and at least seen what they can do.

Sgt. Foster: The only problem I have with all of the girls is that they all think you can't win if you are on the bottom position.

Sgt. Lopez: We will demonstrate how wrong all of you are. Sgt. Foster, let's go to the middle of the ring and show the girls that an elbow lock can send the opponent flying into pin position or at least where you can escape and get back to your feet. Why don't you take the bottom and take me down. Mira Brinson, we will need you to officiate and clap your hands when we are both ready to wrestle. (The two pair up with Sgt. Foley on the bottom and are ready. As Mira claps her hands, Sgt. Foley quickly locks Sgt. Lopez's elbow and rolls Virginia across her back. The two struggle and roll out of bounds on the mat and everybody is amazed at the quickness and strength of the two.) Nice throw Sgt. Foster:, now do all of you think the bottom position is an automatic loss?

Sgt. Foster: Great recovery Sgt. Lopez. Let's pair the girls off and show more basic moves.

Sgt. Lopez: (After observing the girls for awhile, Virginia calls them together.) OK girls, we have had a good workout, but we need to take a short break and come back.

Deirdre: Dallas, it's 10:30, can we see how sweaty Caesar is?

Dallas: Why not, I need to meet Mr. Hot stuff. Let's get going. By the way, did my pointers help out?

Deirdre: In a big time way, thank you. I had the greatest night of my life. When Caesar went to the bathroom, I completely undressed and wrapped up under a blanket. We started out slowly just kissing, and then we kissed and touched all over several times. Even though Caesar didn't tell me when his big moment was, I still tasted some and it wasn't bad. The second time it went all over my chest and I used a hanky to dry it up. Caesar is neat to watch before he explodes, he really squirms and moans. The other day when I touched him down low by the creek, he exploded about six feet into the water. He did try to go all the way but I stopped him dead and let him rub it against my stomach until he exploded all over my stomach. The final encounter was the best. We kissed and touched each other in the shower. When Caesar kissed and touched me the orgasm was so intense, I fell to my knees. That's when I returned the favor. Caesar was so excited he exploded without telling me and it wasn't that bad. Caesar apologized, I told him it wasn't that bad and he was forgiven. We curled up on the couch a few hours and tried to clean up. The only embarrassment was when Mr. Castillo found my stained hanky.

Dallas: Don't put that thing in the dirty wash for mom to find. I do my own wash so give it to me. Mom misses nothing and will jump through the roof if she finds something like that.

Deirdre: How did you stop mom from going through your things?

Dallas: Mom and I struck a peace accord about a year ago. Do you remember the day I was running out the door but didn't make it to school?

Deirdre: Although no one ever asked you, what did happen?

Dallas: I hadn't eaten breakfast and was running out the door to catch the bus. Mom tried to shove some pop tarts into my purse and it caught on the door and spilled on the floor. Mom saw two condoms on the floor and was not only horrified, but started to cry. You know how the Catholic Faith views birth control.

Mary: (With tears and crying.) Dallas, you know I love you as much as the others don't you?

Dallas: (With tears in her eyes.) Yes mom, I always knew. (The two embrace.) I love you so much mom.

Mary: We need to start over. I want a mother- daughter relationship that is strong. If I promise not to fight with or punish you, will you tell me the truth?

Dallas: I'm afraid it will hurt.

Mary: At this point, I still need the truth. How long have you been making love? Please hold me and tell me.

Dallas: My first time was about two years ago at the age of fifteen. (Mary cries harder while Dallas holds her and buries her face in Mary's chest.)Why are you crying so badly mom.

Mary: I feel I failed you. I spent more time punishing you than trying to understand you. I should have had discussions with you in this area as you entered womanhood and did nothing. I feel there is time to salvage our relationship, but you will have to want it too.

Dallas: I do in the worst way. I am willing to open my life up to you, but can we make an agreement on privacy?

Mary: We will talk about that over breakfast. After that we can go shopping at the mall. Let's get cleaned up, changed, and on the mend.

Dallas: (After completely changing.) Ready to go mom.

Mary: (Shocked Dallas look so good) Why didn't you wear some of those nice clothes I made you before today?

Dallas: Because before today, I didn't want you to know I liked anything you did. I admit I always tried to get you. That was because of the things we fought about and how we fought without resolving matters. I admit we didn't have a strong relationship. I want the time to count. We need to talk both in the car and at breakfast. We need to talk all day and the rest of our lives. We also need to discuss our last fight about a year and a half ago.

Mary: Before we get started, does breakfast at the Golden Eagle sound good? That gives us about thirty-five minutes to talk.

Dallas: (As the two girls get into the car, Dallas grabs Mary's hand.) Mom, we need to start talking now.

Mary: Certainly, what issue did you want to?

Dallas: Our last big fight that started at the dinner table.

Mary: Dallas, we've had so many of those, which one.

Dallas: The one that you yanked me out of the chair in the living room.

Mary: I faintly remember that and have long forgiven you.

Dallas: (With lots of tears and holding onto mom.) I never forgave myself. I never apologized for telling you I couldn't wait until you died and that you're not my mother. I'm sorry for calling you a child abuser. (Mary holds Dallas while talking and crying.)

Mary: I have cried many days over that and although you broke my heart in a thousand pieces, I forgive you.

Dallas: Mom, I never forgave myself and I just want you to know how much I love you.

Mary: Is my eye liner and makeup running down my face?

Dallas: Yes, and what about mine?

Mary: I'm afraid we will have to fix our makeup. (Both girls fix up in the car.) Are we ready to go this time?

Dallas: I will say only one thing; I never want to fight like that again.

Mary: Neither do I.

Dallas: Are there any issues that you want to clear? My ears are open and I am in a forgiving mood.

Mary: Despite you forgave my use of force, can you forgive me for some of the things I said and for screaming in your ear?

Dallas: I can easily forgive that. We must make sure we don't get into a bad fight again. I will try to speak to you if I have an issue. I will also let you know everything going on in my life. Now for the million dollar question. How can I get you to stop going through my things?

Mary: I will teach you and Danielle how to do your own wash. However, the two of you must remove your things right away and keep your room neat.

Dallas: Do you promise guys I like will be allowed in the house? I was pretty embarrassed when you wouldn't let Eddie in.

Mary: I admit I was a bit tough. I guess I could let him slide. Now I need to ask you a thing or two. Will you attend church with me every week?

Dallas: Mom, I can't stand church. I especially hate the part where I hear how Christ is a stumbling block for Jews. We also seem to hate other Christian Sects. The Catholic Church has a hell of a nerve asking for forgiveness and for world peace when the only people we get along with is other Catholics. I could try for once a month and as well as Christmas and Easter Services.

Mary: Well, let's settle on our C and E services together.

Dallas: Settled, what do you say we finish breakfast and go shopping? If I think of anything else, I will bring it up.

Mary: We will leave shortly to go shopping but remember one thing; part of negotiating is that both sides get to bring issues to the table. I will be mild, let's get out of here. (The girls go to Fashion Bug and Torrid at Neshaminy Mall.) Get what you want and I will pay for it. If I won't like what you have, hide it from me.

Dallas: Mom, don't come over until I tell you, hopefully I will surprise you. I see a few things that will look great. Look around and I'll call you when I'm ready. (About five minutes later Dallas comes walking out of the dressing room.) Mom, come and see.

Mary: My God honey. A well matched blouse handbag and shoes. I love it; I also like the slacks and sweaters you chose.

Dallas: I did get a few things you won't like.

Mary: Just hide them and I will still pay for everything. I never knew we shared anything in common as far as taste in clothing.

Dallas: I love the way you dress and do many things. I had no intention of telling you unless we came to terms. (Talking in a low voice to Mary.) Mom, love was never our problem. You were always there for me. We just didn't like each other's life styles. You know both of us have hard heads.

Mary: You got that one right. Let's pay for everything and go home.

Dallas: (Entering the front door.) I think we had a great day between us and that we can top it. I also want to know more about you and the past heritage of the Karis Family.

Mary: Does this mean you will improve your appearance every day?

Dallas: Mom, I'm still Dallas and have a profile to maintain at school.

Mary: Could you tell me before you leave so I don't have to look at them.

Dallas: Mom, I plan on putting these things on at school and keeping them in my locker. I promise no more holes in my clothes, tie dyed shirts or colored hair. The only things I bought back were the ACDC earrings and Madonna Cross.

Mary: Will you see cleaner boys?

Dallas: Mom, Eddie Driscoll is such a hot thing.

Mary: For our peace treaty, I will let him in.

Dallas: Can I give you the night off? I've been dying to cook a Chicken Devon and have rolls and veggies.

Mary: Maybe I could learn something from you. Just one question. Did your father really say he liked your meatloaf and apple pie better than mine? Are you sure you weren't trying to aggravate me?

Dallas: Mom please don't be mad, it was both. Dad won't tell you. He does like some of my cooking better.

Mary: After all these years, I still love that man.

Dallas: (Talking with Deirdre.) That is the story with my peace treaty with mom.

Deirdre: I want to go all the way with Caesar. I love him and don't want him looking elsewhere for it.

Dallas: Part of the peace treaty with mom rests on my not talking to you about sex. Besides that, you're too young. Make sure that things are right between the two of you and that he really loves you. I wish I'd waited for my first time. Make sure you talk to mom; she is expecting to hear from you now that you are in love. We are at the gym and I need to meet hot stuff. Let's go find him; I still want to talk to you on the way home. Let me ask dad something, I will catch you in a minute. Dad, how are you doing?

Jack: Just fine honey, how are you?

Dallas: I need to know if I can go to a party at Eddie Driscoll's House.

Jack: Did you already ask your mother?

Dallas: No, I wanted to ask you.

Jack: The answer is still no. I got in lots of trouble for letting you over there before.

Dallas: Thanks dad, I needed that.

Jack: Don't mention it honey, you can ask me anything you want.

Dallas: (Finds Deirdre watching Caesar.) Well, isn't he a hunk! Last night must have been.

Deirdre: (Cutting Dallas off with a big smile.) A real good time. Caesar, I can't stay long. You look very busy.

Caesar: I am very busy working out. Can you come over tonight?

Deirdre: I will wait for you at the end of workouts if that is all right.

Caesar: I already discussed it with my father, stay here and we will give you a ride.

Deirdre: Caesar, this is my sister Dallas, Dallas this is my boyfriend Caesar.

Caesar: Pleased to meet you.

Dallas: Pleased to meet you too. I've heard a lot about you. Don't worry, it's all good. I'll see the two of you soon. Remember, next Saturday is mom and dad's 18th anniversary. See if Caesar can come to the lakes with us.

Deirdre: Great idea, I'll check dad and mom.

Sgt. Lopez: OK girls, back to workouts. I need everybody to the mats. Basically, we will talk the rest of the day. That is after we have a match between two girls who have learned their moves today. (Dorothy Brinson and Carol Martel raise their hands.) OK girls, on the whistle come to the center of the mat and wrestle. (Sgt. Lopez blows the whistle and the two begin to struggle to get control and take each other down. Carol throws Dorothy over her leg but Dorothy quickly rolls on top of Carol and has her in a hold for takedown. Carol breaks the hold and tries to press Dorothy to the mat for a pin, but Dorothy rolls Carol off of her and both get to their feet. As the two grapple for control Carol throws Dorothy to her back. As Carol tries to get control of Dorothy on the ground, Dorothy whips her leg over Carol and pulls out of the hold and drives Carol to the mat for a pin. After the two girls get up they shake hands and embrace becoming friends again.) This is what competition is all about. Losing must be done as gracefully as winning. Remember, it is OK to lose as long as you put your best foot forward. I speak to everybody when I say we must be good sports. It is part of competing. Sgt. Foley, Sgt. Foster and I will be teaching it as well as how to war. It's time to head to the shower and home for the day. I recommend showing up and working out for at least a few hours per day because our first competition is in only one month.

Scene Twenty- Seven: A Night for the Girls

Doreen: (After getting home.) Mom, can I have one of my quieter friends over?

Mary: Who do you want over?

Doreen: What about Tracy?

Mary: Why not, the two of you can watch TV, talk, eat snacks and have breakfast in the morning. Remember, Tracy has to go home so we can go to church at 11:00 in the morning.

Doreen: That will be fine, I'll call Tracy now.

Tracy: Hello, who is it?

Doreen: Hi Tracy, its Doreen. Do you want to come over? My parents said you could spend the night if you're allowed.

Tracey: Give me a second. My parents said all right. I'll be over in a few minutes.

Doreen: (Answers the door.) I've got it mom. I know who it is. Come in Tracy. I hope you brought your appetite with you. My mother is cooking Filet Mignon, baked potatoes and string beans. If you don't like that, we have hot dogs and hamburgers.

Mary: Tracey, do you want what is cooking or a hot dog or hamburger?

Tracey: I'll stay with what is cooking.

Doreen: Let's turn on the TV and gab until dinner. After dinner we need to talk about guys. At 8:00 Miami Vice comes on. Don Johnson is so hot we have to see him.

Mary: Now that dinner is over, why don't we take some strawberry shortcake into the living room? It's almost time for Miami Vice.

Doreen: I'm too young for Don but that doesn't mean that I can't watch him and love him.

Tracey: I'm a big fan of his too. I've noticed Bill Parks looks at you a lot and that the two of you talk. Is something going on there?

Doreen: He is the second hottest guy I've ever known. I really think he is cute and nice. He is a wrestler and is a summer league basketball player. Bill has the cutest butt. I'm dying to go out with him and give him a hot kiss.

Tracey: There are two guys I like, you know one of them.

Doreen: Is that Dave Davidson?

Tracey: Yes, he is cute and nice and I need a quiet sort of guy. Right now we are just friends. He is so shy at times I don't think he notices me. The other guy is Mike Alder. He is cute but I don't always believe his stories.

Doreen: Mike Alder is one of those guys who can't tell the truth. If you have the choice, take Dave. He is so nice, besides being your style of guy; he doesn't know how to lie.

Tracey: Rumor has it even in the slow community, that Bill's family is organizing the block party and he wants you to be his special guest.

Doreen: I can't wait for him to ask. Do you want me to talk to Dave? At times he doesn't get the message until you sit on his head or throw yourself at him.

Mary: (Hearing Doreen's last line.) That may be true but it isn't nice to say that about one of your best friends. Aren't the two of you a bit young to be plotting romance?

Doreen: Mom this is important. I'm eleven years old and plotting a good romance starts now.

Jack: (Laughing in the background.) Honey, take your time. You get plenty of kisses from your mother and me.

Doreen: Dad, that isn't the same as kissing a boyfriend!!! I don't get excited by kissing you. I love you but it isn't the same.

Mary: (With a smile.) Can't you wait a few years?

Doreen: No mom, I have to fall in love and kiss a boy. I'm the only girl in the house who hasn't kissed a boy, been out on a date, or fallen in love. Tracey and I have a number of options to be looked at.

Mary: Tracey, David is the better of the two boys you were speaking of. Speaking of falling in love, it is our eighteenth anniversary and we will be spending the weekend at the lakes. If you want to bring Tracey, you can.

Doreen: Are the Davidsons going to be there?

Mary: Yes, you may be with them for awhile. Daddy and I want to be alone for awhile. Let's pull the bed out so the two of you can watch TV, eat snacks and sleep out here. (In the morning Mary cooks a big breakfast.) We have to get ready for church. Tracey, we will be back later.

Tracey: Thank you for having me over and inviting me along next weekend.

Jack: (Getting home from church.) Honey, Doreen and I are going to the gym and workout.

Mary: OK honey, I'll see you and Doreen when you get home. (Mary calls Laura about the houseboat rentals.)

Scene Twenty-Eight: Planning the Eighteenth Anniversary

Laura: Hello, who is it?

Mary: Hello, its Mary. How have you been?

Laura: Fine, and how is everything with you?

Mary: As you know, our eighteenth anniversary is coming this Saturday. I was wondering where you and Bill got that houseboat for the weekend. I was also wondering if you and Bill can watch the kids Saturday Night. Who did you contact for the rental?

Laura: We will be glad to take the kids. The club owns two houseboats. Penn Warner does one night rentals. Make sure you call them early in the week. Most of the time the boats are rented by late week and they are always rented over the weekends. Make sure you put the mosquito nets down at dusk, they are horrible at night. As you are already know, the view of the stars is fantastic from the shoreline. Viewing the stars while making love on the water is even better.

Mary: Give me the details.

Laura: Why not, Bill and I needed an escape last month and I thank you for watching the boys. Bill and I had dinner and decided to move the boat out of Motorboat cove. Wanting more privacy, we moved the boat to Pike Alley. We anchored about ten feet off one of the islands. We took an evening swim and showered. After that Bill surprised me with a bottle of Bollinger Champagne. We moved two futons together to do some star gazing on the back deck. It was a clear night with a warm gentle breeze. We turned all the lights out and lit candles on the deck. As Bill poured the champagne we looked into each other's eyes as though we just met. The mood was so romantic we started kissing. Bill and I made love on the open deck as though it was our first time. The boat gently rocked as we made love all night. The clubhouse isn't open today, but I would call first thing Monday morning. There is a large and small houseboat, look at both before you choose and have a great weekend.

Mary: Thank you very much, I'll be there tomorrow.

Joan: (The next morning.) Hello, Penn Warner Clubhouse, how can I help you?

Mary: Hello Joan, its Mary.

Joan: Good to hear from you Mary. How are things?

Mary: Everything is fine. I'm inquiring about the houseboat rentals. Are they open for the weekend and can I look at both?

Joan: You're in luck but that won't last.

Mary: Can I look at both boats today?

Joan: Why not, I have very little to do until noon.

Mary: I'll be up in about twenty to thirty minutes. (Mary arrives at the office.) Good morning, how are you Joan?

Joan: I'm fine thank you, grab a cup of coffee and come with me. Toni, watch the office while Mary and I view the rental houseboats.

Mary: In our eight years here, I never knew the houseboats were in Motorboat Cove.

Joan: Well, you never needed one before. If you don't mind my asking, what is the occasion?

Mary: Saturday is our eighteenth anniversary and a chance to get away for the night. I need a one night rental. The kids will be camping with the Davidsons for the night.

Joan: Bill and Laura are good people; your kids are in good hands and will have fun. Let's go on board and look at both. They both have mosquito nets if both of you like the open air and star gazing. Here are your differences; the small boat has more outer deck space. If you like a large cabin and living quarters, take the large boat. Both have a kitchen, living room and bathroom with a shower. Both have futons to lie on as well as rafts and chairs. There is also a ladder to the water to go swimming, we have it all.

Mary: I will take the small boat. My husband and I love the open air.

Joan: The only way I can reserve the boat is if you put a deposit down early.

Mary: I plan on paying for it now.

Joan: Let's go back to the clubhouse. (At the clubhouse.) OK, which night will you need the boat?

Mary: We will take it Saturday Night.

Joan: That will be $125.00 for the night. I also suggest that you take the optional $5.00 insurance policy in case any damage happens to the boat or anybody gets hurt.

Mary: What is the worst thing that happened?

Joan: Two years ago a drunk and stoned idiot ran the boat into the barge in Pike Alley when he fell asleep at the wheel. Had the idiot taken the insurance, he wouldn't have owed us $78, 000.00. See what $5.00 can do for you. I highly suggest you take it.

Mary: I'll take it; I can hardly wait to get my husband alone.

Joan: Why, you bad girl, you. Have a happy eighteenth anniversary. My husband and I celebrated our twentieth back in May. We went to the Pocono's and had a great time. We generally don't do this, but we can tie the boat up or anchor it anywhere you want. This way all you have to do is get a ride to the boat and we will get it later the next day.

Mary: We own our own boat and Bill will probably take us there. If you would, anchor us off the most romantic island in Pike Alley.

Joan: We will do that Saturday morning, when will you be boarding?

Mary: About 1:00PM, if I get a few things, can you make sure they are on board?

Joan: I certainly will. Just make sure you see me before 3:00PM on Friday because we close early in the fall.

Mary: We will see each other on Friday Morning.

Joan: (Thursday morning Mary calls Joan.) Hello, Penn Warner Club, can I help you?

Mary: Hello there, Joan, just a friendly reminder and confirmation of our meeting tomorrow morning.

Joan: Are you bringing anything entertaining?

Mary: I'll show you when I get there. In eighteen years my husband and I haven't had a day or night alone together. He doesn't know what he is in for. It will be the night of our lives.

Joan: Don't forget a good champagne or wine.

Mary: I already got a Dom Perignon and a White Zinfandel. I also got a nice bikini and undergarments. It will be a night we never forget. Will you be there at 9:00AM?

Joan: Yes, if you can stick around we'll go out in the boat and find a perfect spot to anchor the houseboat.

Mary: Why not, we will take care of business tomorrow.

Joan: I will see you tomorrow.

Mary: (With a big smile on Friday Morning.) Hello Joan, I've got quite a collection.

Joan: My goodness you do, between the wine and champagne, you're off to a great start.

Mary: If you think that is something, look at what I bought to wear.

Joan: (Mary opens a night bag.) Oh my god is that man in trouble. A see-through night gown, black French Lace Bra, black stockings and garter belt and skinny black underwear. Why don't we take a ride to Pike Alley and find your perfect location? Let's grab some coffee and go. (Getting to the Pike Alley Sites.) That large beautiful area we are entering is the Driscoll's campsite. There is never a dry or sober moment there.

Mary: I know the Driscolls, they are partiers from the word go. I haven't seen this end of Van Sciver Lake and I love it. Some of my girls wander a bit and may have, though. One of the Davidson boys may have seen it too.

Joan: Dave Davidson and your daughter Dallas know that campsite well.

Mary: What, my oldest daughter and Dave Davidson stop here? I'll put a stop to that. This area is so beautiful that it's a shame the Driscolls have it.

Joan: I'll let you in on a little secret; Mr. Driscoll is the ass that sank the boat. Please keep that to yourself. We are now entering Pike Alley itself which is quite large. What a lot of people like to do is anchor about ten feet off shore from one of the islands. The water is very deep so watch yourself swimming. The fishing is great here so prepare for company during the day. You will be alone at night.

Mary: I like the back of the first island. It is a beautiful wooded area on the island and seems well hidden. I can see the barge Dave and Doreen speak of. I plan on asking those two what they really do when they come here.

Joan: Remember one thing, put the mosquito nets up before dark or your night will be ruined. Have a happy eighteenth anniversary. We will have the boat where you want it and ready to board by 9:00AM.

Mary: Let's head home, I have to pack and be ready to be here this evening.

Joan: (After docking the speed boat.) Enjoy your anniversary.

Mary: (Calling Jack at work.) Hello handsome, how are you doing?

Jack: Great, especially knowing our anniversary will be here. I wish you and I could get away for the day but we can't have it all.

Mary: We do have a boat and I would like to get away for a couple hour cruise after midnight. Maybe we could repeat the first time we made love. Things will be so exciting and new I wish we were already there.

Jack: Make sure we have the citronella candles burning in several places so we aren't food for the mosquitoes. I will make sure there are plenty of pillows, blankets and if you want it, some wine or champagne to celebrate.

Mary: That sounds great; I'll enjoy our celebration under the stars.

Jack: Mary, do the girls know we are heading to the lakes this weekend?

Mary: Yes, the girls can't wait. I allowed them to bring friends. Now that I can trust Dallas, she and Danielle will keep an eye on things.

Jack: How many other people are coming?

Mary: Four other girls are coming. Nadine just called and she thought it was too early for these two to spend a night together. She was nice about it and I agreed. Nadine said she will bring him tomorrow. I think the whole Castillo family will be there tomorrow. Deirdre is a little upset but will get over it. I will get busy packing so we can leave. Did you want to eat at the lakes or home after a shower and change?

Jack: Let's eat at home. Cook hot dogs and hamburgers. We can always cook more after setting camp.

Mary: I love you and will see you about 3:30, please don't be late.

Jack: I love you and won't be late. (As Jack gets home.) I know it's a bit premature, but happy anniversary. (The two share a deep look and a hot kiss.) Wow, you already packed the car and fed the kids. (Jack quickly showers, changes and eats.) Before we all scatter, I want to give your mother her card and present.

Mary: Honey, I would rather do that at the campsite. Right now we are too rushed. Dallas, we need you to drive the family car. There are four other people coming with us.

Dallas: Are you or dad coming with me?

Mary: No, you are on the trusted list until you prove otherwise. Your father and I have some plans to discuss. Follow us to the site. We have to set camp up before dark. (On the way to the campsite.) Honey, I understand Dave Davidson and Dallas visit the Driscoll's campsite frequently. So I don't ruin the weekend, should I make mention that certain campsites like the Driscoll's are off limits? Do you think Dallas is sneaking off to see Eddie and do drugs? Eddie's father better not get any ideas. Did you know David has been there and he is only eleven years old? These things must stop!!!

Jack: What you say doesn't surprise me. Make a mention and I will back you. The two of you have fought enough for a lifetime. We can speak to Bill and Laura about David tomorrow. Mr. Thomas Driscoll is a suspected drug dealer and maker of X- rated movies.

Mary: Rumor has it that the Driscolls sleep around on each other. She has been known to sleep with underage teenage boys.

Jack: Those rumors are true. Both have been known to sleep with teens and to serve drinks and drugs to minors. The department is currently working up a case against the two of them. We also suspect Thomas Driscoll of being a major drug dealer. Some time this weekend, show me where that campsite is, he may be dealing from that location. The two also sold a child pornography film to an under cover cop which they will be arrested for. The film features him sleeping with a girl we believe to be under the age of 18. I know we can at least arrest him. There are five children out of that marriage and they are the same as the adults. All are partiers and enjoy loose sex. I understand the Driscoll's enjoy watching each other have sex with other people.

Mary: I wish someone would arrest those two and give those kids a decent home. (After setting up camp.) OK girls, there won't be many rules this weekend. Your father and I may slip out for awhile this evening. That may happen around 11:00PM. I want everybody to stay at the campsite. Dallas and Danielle will be in charge. The next issue is a warning to stay away from the Driscoll's campsite. A number of you have been seen there. No punishment will be handed out for past actions, but will for new offences.

Danielle: Who told on me?

Mary: You told on yourself, your name wasn't bought up.

Daisy: It had to be Joan.

Mary: It looks like all of you may be guilty. Just don't go there any more. We should drop this before I change my mind.

Dallas: OK mom, we get the message. Can we light a fire and roast marshmallows?

Mary: That's the best idea I've heard yet. Jack, let's get the snacks out.

Jack: Don't mind if I do. Honey, show me what you want in the boat. (As Jack gets back from the van.) OK ladies, let's get this fire lit. If anybody is still hungry, we have hot dogs, hamburgers and marshmallows.

Danielle: Dad, can I light the fire?

Jack: Get the lighter fluid and let's get started. To our four guests, have you eaten? Growing girls can't live on marshmallows alone.

Deirdre: (A little choked up.) Mom, why couldn't Caesar come?

Mary: (Hugging her unhappy daughter.) Honey, Mrs. Castillo called me early today. She thinks Caesar is too young to spend the night with a young lady at this time. Please don't hate her, when you become a parent, you will understand. The whole Castillo family will be visiting tomorrow. I paid for four visitor passes through tomorrow night. Mrs. Castillo did apologize for the last minute decision.

Deirdre: (Deirdre smiles and hugs her mom back.) At least I get to see him tomorrow, I love you mom.

Mary: I love you too, let's get something to eat. (After eating a real meal.) Let's roast some marshmallows; I bought some chocolate bars if anybody wants smores.

Dallas: Mom, can I take a walk after dinner?

Mary: (With a smile.) As long as it isn't the Driscoll's Campsite. I know David goes there too.

Dallas: (All the girls look at each other.) Mom, that campsite is at least a thirty minute walk around the lake.

Mary: (Smiling at Dallas.) So what might you be doing on this walk?

Dallas: (Starting to laugh.) If you take everybody that wants to go, I'll OK it.

Doreen: Let's all go, there are some fun spots.

Dallas: (Rolling her eyes in the air.) All right, everybody can come.

Danielle: (Whispering to Dallas.) Are you meeting Eddie Driscoll or hanging out at the Johnson's Campsite? I really like Bobby. I know you dated Andrew and it didn't work. Do you think you could introduce me to a real fox?

Dallas: It so happens I am meeting Eddie at the Johnson's campsite. I hoped to go there alone, but everybody can come. If Bobby is there, I will introduce you to him. I don't know if he is seeing anybody. I will tell you this: Bobby treats a girl a lot better than Andrew. All Andrew does is sleep around, but if he ever grows up, I would like to go out with him again.

Danielle: Do you still love Andrew?

Dallas: I will never stop loving Andrew. He is very immature and lives for three things only: His next screw, drugs and drinking. I hope he grows up, but it isn't likely.

Danielle: Do you know anything about Bobby?

Dallas: Yes, he is the kind of man every girl should have. I hear he is good in bed, dependable and stays with one girl when he gives himself to her.

Danielle: What was the final straw that made you call everything off?

Dallas: Andrew has several years on me. I was a sophomore in high school when he asked me to the senior prom. Andrew was an hour late when I called his house. When I asked where he was, Mr. Johnson said he went to the prom. When I told him Andrew was supposed to take me, he said Andrew went with a date and I must be mistaken. I cried all night, mom made me a better gown than I could have rented. As bad as our relationship was, mom felt sorry for me. She helped me to dry my tears and make my decision to drop him. Hot guys are all I wanted; little did I realize they are full of lies and empty promises. If Bobby is there and you can attract him, you will be a lucky girl.

Danielle: Why can't you get over anybody who was rotten to you? You can't live your life waiting for Andrew to straighten up.

Dallas: Even though I date other guys, I would drop them all if Andrew would straighten up. I always got the feeling I was somebody when I was with him. My spine tingles when he is near me. Andrew left a real impression on me and is my first love. He is also my first broken heart. Eddie Driscoll is my second. The two families share one thing in common; they are full of good times and shit. There is never a dull moment. All of the males are rotten to the women. The good one is Bobby.

Danielle: Let's wait for Dave Davidson. Doreen and Tracy want him with us. Do you think mom will tell on Dave?

Dallas: I hope not, but you know it will slip out.

Danielle: Was Dave over the Driscoll's Campsite?

Dallas: Yes, he was there when I babysat the Davidson's at there campsite. Tommy had to go to the hospital over a bad cut on his foot. Laura came over and asked me to watch Dave who couldn't sleep. I wanted to get high with Eddie. His younger sister Belinda who had friends over playing spin the bottle. Belinda had to kiss Dave. Belinda who is fourteen was drunk and stoned, didn't know Dave was only eleven years old. She not only kissed Dave in the game, she made out with Dave after the game and touched him between the legs. She asked Dave to sleep with her but he turned her down. Dave and Belinda made out several times since then. Belinda said had she known his age she wouldn't have done it. Belinda admitted she fooled around with Dave and gave him an orgasm although they didn't go all the way. Belinda said she knew something was wrong when she had to tell him how to touch and hold her to make her feel good.

Danielle: How did you know these things went on?

Dallas: I was getting ripped and laid with Eddie. I have been there and found Dave visiting. When Belinda asked his age she was shocked and said she will have to stop seeing him. I feel terrible about introducing them; please say nothing about what I told you. Mom and Laura will never trust me again.

Danielle: Looks like Dave is here, let's gather everybody and go.

Dallas: One thing we have to do is keep the younger kids occupied. I will be spending some time with Eddie. We have to keep the kids out of the party zone tent where everybody goes to get drunk, stoned and laid. We can take shifts watching them.

Danielle: We have to keep them from spin the bottle.

Dallas: We will take shifts watching them by the water. Daisy and Darlene can watch them for awhile although we all take turns.

Scene Twenty-Nine: It's off to Party.

Dallas: OK everybody let's get moving. (Dallas looks at Andrew after getting to the Johnson's Campsite.) Well look at what the wind blew in.

Andrew: How are you doing?

Dallas: Everything is fine; I have a few things to ask you.

Andrew: What may those things be?

Dallas: Is Bobby seeing anybody?

Andrew: Bobby just got his heart broken. He is alone by the water but will be OK.

Dallas: Have you seen Eddie?

Andrew: Yes, but you may not like it. Eddie came here with somebody else. I don't know if she is his girlfriend.

Dallas: (Seeing Eddie getting out of the tent adjusting his pants up and kissing another girl begins to cry.) I think I will leave and find the only real man here.

Andrew: What about me?

Dallas: (With a nasty look.) Yeah, what about you? Oh that's right; I didn't include you in the category of good man. If you ever grow up, I may include you. (Dallas turns her back and walks to the water with Danielle.) Hello Bobby, how have you been?

Bobby: Lousy, I just lost a great girl. My heart is so broken I feel like I'm going to die.

Scene Thirty: Love at First Sight

Dallas: Hang tough, things like this take time to heal. One of the cures is finding somebody who cares. Do you mind if I introduce you to my sister? Bobby, this is my sister Danielle. Danielle, this is Bobby.

Danielle: Are you the guy I always see on one ski flying around at about 50 MPH? Do you jump from the ramp in Pike Alley?

Bobby: I am that guy. Do you like waterskiing, rafting, boating and swimming?

Danielle: I enjoy water sports.

Bobby: How come I haven't met you yet?

Danielle: I don't get around like Dallas does.

Bobby: I know all of your sisters. Come down with us, we have a lot of fun. Dallas, did you bring kids down here at night; you know you shouldn't do that.

Dallas: It's the only way we got to come.

Bobby: Danielle, let's get a beer and come back to the water. We can talk and watch the kids together. Dallas, Eddie appears free if you want to talk to him.

Dallas: Just one question, do you know if he had sex with the girl I saw walking out of the tent?

Bobby: Odds are with it he did. They have been kissing and holding each other all day.

Dallas: Is her name Cathy Roper?

Bobby: Yes, she is the class slut. She had the whole football and wrestling team in bed at least once. Cathy and Eddie are meant for each other.

Dallas: (With a hard disgruntled look.) I will deal with those two later. Right now I need a beer. (Smiling as she passes Eddie.) How are you stranger?

Eddie: Fine, and how are you?

Dallas: Who were you partying with? Are you going out with somebody new?

Eddie: Cathy and I are friends.

Dallas: Watch yourself; I hear she is a slut.

Eddie: She means nothing to me.

Dallas: Get a beer and join us. I have to watch the kids so watch what you pull out in front of them.

Eddie: I'd like to join you; do you think we could slip away for awhile?

Dallas: That is why I came here. I just introduced Danielle to Bobby Johnson and they went to get a beer.

Eddie: Wow, hooking your sister up with Bobby Johnson. Come to think of it, they are a pair.

Dallas: I hope it's a fit. Both deserve somebody nice. (After arriving by the water.) OK guys, we'll see you in a minute. All of you can wade or sit on the dock, but no swimming. As for you Eddie, I have plans for you. (With the two smiling at each other, Dallas gives Eddie a short hot kiss.) A little later and we'll slip away and party. Right now we have kiddie watch.

Eddie: (Eddie whispers to Dallas.) If you're horny, I have a rubber.

Dallas: Sorry, but it's the wrong time of month. We can do everything but go all the way. (The two have a steamy French kiss.) Down boy down.

Eddie: I can't help myself when I get started. You don't know what you do to me. Watch one of the kids is starting for the water.

Dallas: Dave, Tracey and Doreen, get away from the water.

Tracy: (With a smile.) Just needed to see if you are awake.

Dallas: Please don't test me like that again.

Doreen: "Yes mom", where is Danielle?

Dallas: Getting something to drink.

Doreen: Is Danielle going out with Bobby?

Dallas: Not yet, but hopefully soon. Don't start with her like you did with Deirdre, I want this to work.

Doreen: I see them getting something to drink.

Danielle: Do you drink often?

Bobby: No, I don't even go to most of the parties. When I have a girlfriend, I like to spend my time with her. I even have a different set of friends. These guys are all right, but there is never a dry moment.

Danielle: I'll let you in on a secret; this is my first beer ever.

Bobby: (With a little snicker.) Every here and there it's fun to drink. The thing you have to watch is that you don't get too drunk.

Danielle: (Gives Bobby an eye to eye smile.) If I get drunk, will you walk me home? If I get drunk, please be a gentleman and don't take advantage of me.

Bobby: (Smiling at Danielle.) Even if you ask me to, I promise not to take advantage of you. I can see you are a little shy, but stop worrying; I'm not one of the cool crowd.

Danielle: So you like quiet girls. When you're out with a girl, would you rather be alone or with a crowd? My last few boyfriends always wanted their friends around. I like going out and having people around, but those things have their time and place.

Bobby: I haven't found anybody like you yet. We think on the same line. (The two move closer and Bobby put his arm around Danielle.) Let's call the kids over and have a marshmallow roast. The kids will be with us so Dallas and Eddie can slip away. Before we do that, I would like to toast a wonderful and beautiful night with great company.

Danielle: (Danielle quickly kisses Bobby off the lips after toasting him.) Will I see you again or is this just a dream?

Bobby: You will see me tomorrow. Let me walk you back to your campsite later and I will come over tomorrow. Let me kiss you. (The two lock up in a steamy kiss.) Let's call the kids over now.

Dallas: Eddie, do you remember when we kissed like that as a couple? Why do I only get that sort of thing with you when I'm not dating anyone? Are you sure you're not just screwing Cathy Roper? Please don't lie to me; I'm tired of just having sex with you. I would like to start seeing you seriously again but don't know if I can trust you. Bobby is the type that stays with a girl. At least Danielle stands a chance if she can land him. We have to be back around 10:00 because my parents want to get lost awhile for their eighteenth anniversary. (Danielle sees Eddie and Dallas lock up in a hot kiss.)

Danielle: Why don't the two of you get lost for awhile?

Eddie: Not a bad idea. (The kids are called over to the fire.)

Bobby: Who wants to roast marshmallows? (Everybody comes over.)

Doreen: Let's get some sticks, I want to roast marshmallows and we don't have long.

Scene Thirty-One: Farewell my Love

Belinda: Where is Dave?

Doreen: Is he your boyfriend? Did you know he is only eleven years old?

Belinda: I didn't know, but I have to talk to him.

Tracy: Let Dave alone. I will only tell you where he is if you are breaking up with him.

Belinda: I'm ending it tonight, where is he?

Tracy: Right behind you, gathering sticks.

Belinda: Dave, I need to talk to you, let's go to the tent.

Dave: I know what this talk will be. (The two close the tent flap s and tie them shut. Both loosen their clothes and begin kissing and touching all over.)

Belinda: (Whispers softly in Dave's ear as Belinda is kissing and touching him.) This is the last time we can touch each other. Let's enjoy each other's company. Put your hands on me and kiss me all over. It feels so good, it feels so damn good. Don't stop, it feels so good, AHHHH AHHHH AHHHH!!!!. (Belinda moaned so loud it could be heard outside the tent.)

Dave: (As Belinda begins to get excited her body quivers uncontrollably and she tightens her hold on Dave. Dave whispers softly.) Belinda, hold me tighter and kiss me some more. Keep going, hold tighter and pull faster. (Dave begins to hold tighter and kiss harder.) Belinda, you make me feel so good.

Belinda: (With Dave holding on as tight as he can, Belinda lowers her head and finishes the love session.) I enjoyed our time together.

Dave: Belinda, you make me feel so good. If you're going to break my heart, get it done now.

Belinda: I would like to be friends but can't see you romantically anymore.

Dave: OK, I understand.

Belinda: Where are you going?

Dave: Back to the fire.

Belinda: Don't you care?

Dave: Not at all.

Belinda: Bastard, and to think I had some of my hottest moments with you.

Dave: This wasn't just sex, I really like you and will remember you the rest of my life. (Belinda cries as Dave goes back to his friends.)

Scene Thirty-Two: Dallas Gets Revenge.

Dallas: It's our turn to go to the tent Eddie.

Eddie: Why can't we make love?

Dallas: Because it's the wrong time of month, but we can touch each other and feel good together. (Dallas softly whispers in Eddie's ear.) Don't you want the best oral sex and touch session you've ever had? We can do everything but make love.

Eddie: Let's go to the tent. (Once they get inside the tent, the two of them close the flaps, tie them shut and begin to aggressively make out.) Loosen your clothes, I want to kiss and touch you all over.

Dallas: (With her senses completely turned on and both hearts pounding.) Keep touching me, keep touching me all over. (Dallas orders Eddie.) Keep touching me and kissing me all over. (Dallas begins to lose control.) You're driving me nuts. It's so good, it's so god damn good. (Dallas begins kissing and touching Eddie. Heavy breathing can be heard outside the tent. When reaching down, Dallas notices Eddie is wet to the touch.) Eddie, you're so excited, lay back and enjoy this.

Eddie: Keep going, you make me feel so good. (Before Eddie lays back Dallas whispers in his ear.) I know you sleep with Cathy. (As Eddie lays back, Dallas begins to lower her head, she grabs Eddie hard and yanks him. Eddie screams at her at the top of his lungs.) Ouch, you lousy bitch, why did you hurt me like that?

Dallas: (Yelling at Eddie.) You bastard, you had unprotected sex with a known slut like Cathy Roper, didn't wash up, and ask me for sloppy seconds. (Dallas slaps Eddie's face hard with her wet hand and continues to yell at Eddie.) Take that you low life. Don't you ever speak to me again?

Eddie: Burn in hell bitch.

Bobby: (Looks at Danielle as she and all of the kids start laughing.) What was that about?

Danielle: (Laughing while explaining.) My sister is getting even with Eddie for cheating on and breaking up with her.

Bobby: Remind me not to piss her off.

Doreen: Yeah, Dallas is mean.

Dave: Don't get into a war with that one.

Danielle: (Snuggles up to Bobbie and talks to Dallas.) What did you do to Eddie, we all heard him scream.

Dallas: That bastard wanted me for sloppy seconds and didn't even wash up after sleeping with a slut. I took my good time and left him in pain in several places.

Doreen: Where did you leave him in pain?

Dallas: You're too young to know.

Doreen: Where are you going?

Dallas: To the lake to wash my hands.

Bobby: Wait a minute Dallas; I will get you some soap.

Danielle: Dallas, we have some sticks if you want to roast some marshmallows.

Dallas: I will join you in a minute, and then Dallas lays a nasty set of eyes on Dave. (An authoritative tone.) What were you doing with Belinda? She better have broken up with you.

Dave: She did, I expected it.

Dallas: Did you have sex again?

Dave: Yes, it was the last time.

Dallas: I will kill that bitch tomorrow, go back to the fire.

Dave: I'll see you when you get back.

Dallas: (After an hour of roasting marshmallows.) OK everybody, it's time to go. Mom and dad will be waiting for us.

Bobby: (After a few beers.) Danielle, you look a little woozy.

Danielle: I can barely walk; does this mean I'm a sloppy drunk or a floozy?

Bobby: No, it means you're a cheap date. Let me walk you home. (As everybody gets back to the campsite, Mary is waiting by the tent.)

Danielle: Bobby, kiss me goodnight. (Mary sees the two have a nice kiss.) Come by tomorrow morning.

Bobby: I don't want to bother your family early. I'll come around 10:00 in the morning.

Mary: (Walks around the tent and invites Bobby to join them.) Why don't you come around 7:00 and have breakfast with us? If you would like to help us catch breakfast, come about 5:00AM. Oh yes, I'm Danielle's mother, Mary, who are you?

Bobby: (The two shake hands.) I'm Bobby Johnson; it's nice to meet you. I will come by early and help catch breakfast.

Mary: (With a smile.) I will get to know you tomorrow. Have a good night.

Bobby: I will see you early, have a good night.

Mary: Is he one of the Johnsons who normally parties with the Driscolls?

Danielle: (With some reserve.) Yes, does that mean I can't see him?

Mary: (With a smile.) No, it surprised me he was polite and not really drunk or stoned. I will only watch him a little. I know he's the only one of the Johnsons not in trouble with the law. He is the only one of the Johnsons allowed in the house.

Danielle: How do you know so much about him?

Mary: Your father is in charge of the juvenile department. I know all about the kids you and your sisters hang out with. You and Dallas are in charge of camp while your father and I go out in the boat.

Scene Thirty-Three: A Celebration under the Stars.

Danielle: I hope it is as beautiful a night under the stars for the two of you as it has been for me. The kids won't be in any trouble. I want to wish you a happy anniversary before midnight.

Mary: (Hugs Danielle and calls Jack.) Jack, guess what time it is? Let's get into the boat and go handsome.

Jack: I was just getting a few things, let's get out of here.

Mary: So what did you get me.

Jack: Not until after midnight and celebration.

Mary: Celebration may go better with some wine or champagne and exchange of presents and cards.

Jack: Let's go to Pike Alley and tie up to a tree so we can take care of those things. (Jack unties the line and shoves off.) I love you so much. (Mary sits on Jack's lap.) Did you want to pour some wine for the ride? (They look at each other and kiss.) We are leaving Motorboat Cove; watch out how you distract me. The channel is narrow and we need to make it into the main lake water before we do what we want.

Mary: (Still in the channel Mary pours the wine, they toast and kiss.) I didn't hear what you said. (Mary softly blows in Jack's ear.)

Jack: (With some emphasis.) Honey, watch that!!! I could run aground here. You still have what it takes to put a chill down my spine.

Mary: I would like to propose a toast to eighteen great years, may there be many more.

Jack: I'll toast to that. (The two toast as they enter the main lake.) Time for the exchange.

Mary: (Loves her card and present.) Jack, the words in this card, especially where you wrote are wonderful. Now let's see what you got me. (With a deep breath.) This is beautiful, a past, present and future necklace.

Jack: I noticed you liked it so I bought it.

Mary: Now it's your turn, everything is in the card and I hope you like it.

Jack: Honey, I love this card. Looks like an invite inside. Oh my God, you rented a houseboat for the evening, I love it, where and when?

Mary: Tomorrow night although our trip starts tomorrow afternoon. It's already set that the boat I rented will be anchored about ten feet off the first island in Pike Alley. I have plans for a quiet private night together.

Jack: I can hardly wait. How are we getting out there and what about the kids?

Mary: Bill will take us out there in our boat. The Davidsons will watch the kids; I've had this worked out for about a week.

Jack: I love the way your mind works, you can be so bad, then again, and that's when you're so good.

Mary: Now that we don't have to watch as much, I want to toast a warm and beautiful evening and a happy anniversary. (The two toast.) Kiss me fool. (The two break into deep kissing. Mary blows softly into Jack's ear and softly nibbles on his ear lobes. Mary pulls her pants down then she pulls Jack's pants down.) Celebration begins now, keep steering the boat. This is a test of your navigational skills while distracted. (Mary grabs Jack's throbbing flesh.) Your test begins now. (Mary works Jack's erect penis until it stands tall. Then she begins going down on Jack taking him deep down her throat while massaging the shaft with her hand and tongue.)

Jack: (In a low voice.) You're so good to me. (While stroking her hair.) I love you so much. (Mary lifts her head and sits on Jack's throbbing flesh.) Move your hips slowly honey. (Jack gets so excited he has to shut the engine down. The two engage in deep kissing with heavy breathing and probing tongues.) Honey, it feels so good, keep going, and don't stop. (Holding each other tight and breathing heavily.) Honey, I'm going to cum, keep going and hold me tight.

Mary: Let it go Jack, cum inside of me honey. I love you so much. (Highly excited, Jack explodes inside of Mary.) This isn't anywhere near over. I want you on the floor. (Lying on the floor, Mary pulls her legs back.) Put it in honey, I want you so bad.

Jack: Kiss me while I'm loving you. (Grabbing Jack's organ, Mary inserts Jack.) Mary, I feel so good when I love you.

Mary: (Mary directs Jack in a soft voice.) Stroke me slow and deep like you always do. I enjoy it when you're inside honey. (As she enters orgasm, Mary groans and tightens her grip with her arms and legs.)I'm going to love you to the end of time. (Jack strokes Mary another thirty minutes before the boat runs aground.) Finish what you started.

Jack: I'm going to cum honey, hold me tight. (Jack cums deep inside.) I love you, Mary.

Mary: I love you honey. (With a smile and smart tone.) In case you need to know, you failed you're driving while distracted test, but passed you're deep drivers test. Let's get out of here you lousy driver.

Jack: One quick kiss.

Mary: Why is that?

Jack: It's past midnight, happy anniversary. (The two snuggle in a hot deep kiss and shove off for Pike Alley.) Honey, did you pack the citronella candles?

Mary: Yes I did, I also bought a Dom Perignon to bring to our anniversary "party."

Jack: You went all the way.

Mary: For you, it's the only way to go. (When they get to Pike Alley they tie the boat up to a tree on the first island, burn the candles and toast their anniversary.) Jack, I think we are safe to undress, take me to the back seat. (As Mary lies back they begin to slowly make love.) Cum inside honey. (After Jack cums, Mary faces the barge.) Take me from behind; put your hands on my breasts. Make love to me honey, tonight is our night. Push it slow and deep honey, keep going, and keep going honey. (With Jack supporting Mary's breasts, Mary slowly switches her hips and drives Jack nuts.) I'm Cumming like crazy honey, keep going, harder, push it harder and deeper AHHH!!! AHHH!!! Don't stop until you cum.

Jack: Honey, I'm cumming. I love you so must. (After an energized love session the two curl up with pillows, blankets and a fresh glass of champagne.) You're the greatest woman, after all these years, I still don't know what you saw in me. I just want you to know you are the center of my life and one of my big reasons for living.

Mary: (Smiling but shedding tears of joy.) I saw a man that would love me with all of his heart and I needed a man like you who comes home to his family every night. I will love you to the ends of time. (After several drinks the two put their clothes on and go home about 3:00AM.) We need to turn in and get up about 5:00AM.

Jack: With a day of fun as well as a relaxing day ahead, we need some sleep. (The two cuddle up in the same sleeping bag.)

Mary: It's time to get up for coffee and catch breakfast. I want to wait for Bobby Johnson who said he would be here. I'll get Danielle and Doreen up, to.

Jack: Happy anniversary, I had a great night and look forward to an even better one this evening.

Scene Thirty-Four: Bobby Gets the Mom Test

Mary: (Mary spots Bobby Johnson approaching.) Honey, I see Danielle's Prince Charming. I can't believe that one of Daniel Johnson's boys doesn't party much.

Jack: Be easy on him honey. Bobby is the only person in that house who isn't in legal trouble. He works, gets good grades, keeps a low profile, and somehow finds time to be a great athlete and date. Bobby doesn't like his family much. The only thing he does at home is eat and sleep. I hear he finished his first semester at East Stroudsburg University.

Mary: Sounds like a lonely life. He is handsome and seems bright. Unlike the rest of his family, he seems to be picky about his company.

Jack: Whatever you do, don't look for all of his faults. Bobby Johnson is very nice and the only hope for the Johnson Family to show a decent person out of that house. In that respect, I feel badly for him.

Mary: I trust your judgment. Just let me talk to him. I need to get to know my daughter's new boyfriend. (As Bobby shows up.) Well, how are you Bobby Johnson? My daughter is intently waiting for you and probably worried that I am giving you the "mom test." If you would like a cup of coffee and a doughnut head over to the fire then join Danielle. (Mary sees the way Danielle smiles at Bobby as he approaches her and looks into his eyes before they have a short kiss.) Jack, did you see the way they look at each other? I hope this blossoms.

Jack: Part of that will depend on you letting them alone.

Mary: What I did was part of a mother's job. Bobby just passed the mother's test.

Jack: Tell me, have I kissed those soft beautiful lips this morning?

Mary: (With a loving smile.) Quite a few times between the hours of midnight and three in the morning. (The two share a soft kiss.) Happy anniversary, I love you Jack.

Jack: I love you too; let's leave the two of them alone to experience young love.

Mary: Aside from a motherly talk with Danielle, that is what I plan to do.

Bobby: Let's sit on the rocks, cast our lines, get real close and go home with some breakfast.

Danielle: (The two cast and snuggle. Curling up tight, the two kiss nonstop until Danielle comes up for air.) At this rate we won't know if we have a bite.

Bobby: The fish we are after are very big. Trust me we will know. (Bobby's line is pulled very hard.) Here we go, this is a game fish. (After a big fight Bobby lands a big bass.) Wow, this bass must weigh three pounds.

Danielle: Look, my line is getting small tugs.

Bobby: Wait until your line rides out steadily. I bet it's a Walleye. Danielle's line starts to pull out slowly and steadily and begins to speed up.) Wait, wait, don't pull yet. Pull now and keep the tip of your pole up.

Danielle: (With a big fight on her line.) Help me out a little Bobby; it's hard to reel in.

Bobby: You're doing just fine but we don't have a net. I have to climb down to the water. (Bobby grabs the walleye by the gill after the fish tires of fighting and throws it ashore.) What a catch, these two will make a great breakfast.

Danielle: (The two catch five fish for breakfast.) We caught them, who wants to clean them.

Bobby: I'll clean them.

Mary: I have cooking duties, after breakfast we will start boating; waterskiing and rafting so stick around. I know you enjoy all of them.

Danielle: I have things to learn so I will come with you Bobby.

Mary: What about learning more about cooking?

Danielle: You already taught me everything I need to know. (With a laugh looking at mom.) I will see you in a little bit.

Mary: (Smiling in return.) I will see you when you get back.

Jack: (After a good breakfast.) OK guys, who wants to do some boating?

Bobby: Sounds great, I'm in.

Danielle: If you go I go.

Bobby: What I'm looking for is some waterskiing or rafting with a beautiful young lady at my side.

Danielle: I can hardly wait.

Doreen: I heard you won a waterskiing contest; let's see what you can do.

Bobby: Well, right now hogging up time by myself wouldn't be polite and wasn't what I had in mind. When it's time, I would like to ski or raft with that beautiful sister of yours.

Mary: (Whispers to Jack.) I see he is really nice and respects Danielle. I also like the fact that he isn't a showoff. As far as I'm concerned, he is off to a great start.

Scene Thirty-Five: A Day of Fun on the Water.

Jack: Bob, come with me and help me shove off. I have to meet everybody at the docks at Turkey Point. Honey, why don't you pack everybody in the van and meet us there? Bobby, if you and Danielle want to come with me in the boat I will find it easier to dock.

Bobby: I'll be right there.

Danielle: I'm ready to go dad.

Bobby: (Holding Danielle's hand and helping her get on board.) Let's get into the boat. I have to cast lines off so we can get out of here, and then get in to shore.

Jack: OK Bob, untie the lines and let's cast off. That went nice and smooth; I've seen you on the water for years. You're quite a skier and swimmer; I hear you've won competitions. I also hear you recently started college at East Stroudsburg Univ. What are you taking up.

Bobby: Yes, I'm currently a freshman and I'm currently home for the weekend. I'm taking up computer science. I've competitively swam and skied since a junior in high school. I noticed Doreen saw me compete somewhere.

Jack: She always read up on you winning a lot of swim meets in school and she watched you compete on water skies in Florida. You're one of the few kids who have competed on TV at an early age. She loved it when you went over the jumps and when you skied on your bare feet. Doreen and I have seen you do those things here.

Bobby: I learned everything I know by skiing and swimming here. I still practice all of my routines here because of all of the open water space.

Jack: Traveling all over the US to compete must be neat.

Bobby: The competing is fun, but it won't last for ever. That's why I'm perusing computers, they are for ever and I can work anywhere.

Jack: What area of computers are you looking at?

Bobby: The up and coming area of computers is computer repair. There aren't many who want to do it.

Jack: That sounds like a good plan, good luck in your studies. It's time to dock. It won't take long to get ready. Danielle, when we get out, get ready to ski or raft first. Doreen, how would you and Tracy like to ride in the back of the boat and spot these two? You may see some real talent.

Doreen: Why not, this should be fun.

Tracy: When is Dave coming? I'll enjoy watching this; Bobby is so good at skiing and such a stud.

Jack: Knowing how Mr. Davidson sleeps in, he will be down in an hour or two. Mary, let's get into the boat and get some air blown through our hair. Honey, please take the wheel so I can shove us off.

Mary: Does this mean I'm captain.

Jack: Yes, you will do just fine. Doreen and Tracy, make sure you tell me if Danielle or Bobby falls. Do the two of you want to ski or use the raft?

Danielle: The two of us talked it over and want to use the raft.

Bobby: Mr. Bordowski, if you don't mind, we talked it over and want to use one raft.

Jack: That will be just fine. Paddle out about ten feet in the water. Thumbs up means faster, thumbs down means slower. Ok honey, take the boat out and we can circle back and feed them the line.

Bobby: Let's have you ride on my back. Wrap your arms around me and hold on tight. This is the first time I ever went rafting this way. It should be fun.

Doreen: He is such a fox.

Tracy: Bobby is so hot, why can't I be older and in Danielle's place.

Danielle: (Waiting for the rope, Danielle kisses Bobby.)I Love you Bobby, I'll enjoy riding on top of you.

Bobby: Hold on tight and you'll get the ride of your life.

Mary: (After a few hours.) Jack, drop me off on the dock and head back to the campsite. The Davidsons and Castillos will be there. We need to pack and leave in one hour.

Jack: Bobby and Danielle, do the two of you want to come with me so it is easy to tie up?

Bobby: Why not, it will cap a great day. I have to pack and get back to school.

Danielle: Please promise you will come home on the weekends and keep in contact during the week.

Bobby: I will finally have a reason to come home for the weekends. If things go right between us, I will transfer to Penn State Ogontz Campus. I'm about half way through the semester. You are one of the most wonderful girls I've ever met and my only reason for coming home. (The two exchange numbers and addresses before Bobby leaves.)

Danielle: (Holding on to Bobby.) Give me a call at home tomorrow.

Bill: (The Davidson's arrive.) Well, taking a little trip I see.

Mary: Yes, I got the idea from Laura; she said the two of you had a great time.

Bill: It was a reminder of when we were first married and free to do what we wanted. Do the two of you need any help packing?

Mary: No, we only have a few things.

Laura: (Whispering to Mary.) Did you pack a sexy night gown and a bottle of wine or champagne?

Mary: (Whispering to Nancy.) You better believe it. I plan on a lot of time with no clothes on.

Laura: You bad girl, you. I hope this is as good for the two of you as it was for us. Is everybody here that is staying?

Mary: No, Deirdre's boyfriend is coming with his mother and possibly the whole family. It didn't sound like they wanted to spend the night. If there is a change of heart, let them spend the night.

Deirdre: (Hugs and kisses Caesar as the Castillo's arrive.) Caesar, I missed you last night. Kiss me or lose me forever, fool. (Caesar kisses Deirdre again.) By the way, Laura Davidson, meet Nadine, Caesar and Denise Castillo.

Laura: Pleased to meet you. We can get to know each other while Bill takes the lovebirds to their destination. When Bill returns, we can swim, water ski, and raft.

Mary: Let's pack and go to the boathouse. The quicker Bill returns, the quicker the fun for the kids resumes.

Jack: (While taking the boat to the destination.) I hear you and Laura had a great time when you did this a few months ago.

Bill: Yes we did. It was more than just a lot of sex. We were free to party and do anything we wanted. We can't thank you and Mary enough for watching the kids. It was a time we will never forget. Hopefully things work the same for you as it did for us. Where is the houseboat anchored?

Mary: Off the first island in Pike Alley. It's nice and quiet there and I get Jack alone. Believe it or not, Jack and I were never alone overnight. I was carrying Dallas and Danielle when we first married. This will be our first night alone together.

Jack: I can't wait to get there. It's time to enjoy life together. (As they approach Pike Alley.) It is so beautiful out here. Honey, did you pack the citronella candles? I don't want to deal with the mosquitoes.

Mary: I brought the candles, but we also have mosquito nets. I was told to put them up an hour before dusk.

Jack: Which boat did you get honey?

Mary: The smaller one. It had a bigger deck. That was the one you said you would take if you had the time and money.

Jack: Bill, we are lucky men with beautiful and observant wives.

Bill: You got that one right. (Bill sees the boat.) They put you in a great spot. Let's tie up, I can help you unpack and go. I couldn't imagine you want company tonight.

Mary: (As Bill is ready to leave.) I can't thank the two of you enough for watching the kids. (Mary kisses Bill off the cheek.)

Jack; (Laughing and kidding with Mary.) Mary, you're supposed to be saving those kisses for me.

Bill: (Also laughing and kidding.) I'm sure she has a lot left. I need to be going. What time would you like to be picked up?

Mary: How about 4:00pm?

Jack: (Laughing all the way.) Four sounds good. By the way Bill, take the flare gun with you. If the kids are trouble send for help. Mary and I won't be there, but will think of you.

Bill: (As he slowly pulls away.) If the kids are bad, you will get them back.

Scene Thirty-Six: Let the Party Begin

Mary: (Takes out a bottle of champagne.) You're in a lot of trouble starting now. Let's go inside and pour some champagne. After that change into your bathing suit, I'm changing into something you'll love.

Jack: (The second the two get inside the cabin, they begin a hot French kiss.) What would that be?

Mary: Ah Ah Ah!!! I'm going to the bathroom to change into something more comfortable. You should get out of those clothes. I'm dying to put this new bathing suit. (Mary changes into a string bikini.)

Jack: (While Mary is changing.) I'm dying to see this new bathing suit.

Mary: Oh Jack, close your eyes. Now open them. This is all you will see until we go home. (The two engage in a hot French kiss.) I love you so much. You're in so much trouble, even you don't know. It's our first night alone in eighteen years. (Rips her bra off.) My breasts are always open for you.

Jack: (Ripping off his bathing suit.) Mary, you're so beautiful, I love you.

Mary: (While kissing him and pulling on Jack's hard penis.) You always get so big and hard, lie back and enjoy it honey.

Jack: (As Mary mounts Jack.) Love always feels so good with you.

Mary: (Inserts Jack in her warm wet tunnel of love.) AHHH! Jack I'm so hot and horny. Lie back and let me do all the work. It feels so good when we make love. (Mary slowly grinds her hips.) AHHH!!! Jack, you're so big and hard. I'm going to cum, I'm cumming honey, I'm cumming so hard.

Jack: (Mary leans forward grimacing, cumming, and quivering.) Put your nipples in my mouth. Keep pushing faster; I'm going to cum too.

Mary: (In the middle of a hard orgasm.) Jack, oh Jack, I'm cumming, I'm cumming so hard. This is the best it's ever been. Hold me real tight and close. (Clutching each other real tight and close Jack explodes inside of Mary.) I'm so excited, let's go for two honey. I love you Jack. Oh god Jack, I'm starting to cum honey, I'm cumming again.

Jack: (Still panting, lies on top of Mary.) If you're not tired, let me have the top. (With the two engaged in a kiss, Jack rolls Mary to the bottom.)

Mary: Jack, don't push hard honey. (Jack begins loving Mary as directed; she begins breathing hard and whispers in Jack's ear.) Jack, you're always so big and hard. Push it slow and deep. (In a hard orgasm Mary tightly wraps her legs around Jack's back.) I love you Jack, I love you. I'm cumming, I'm cumming again. (Mary pulls her knees straight back.) Keep pushing, keep pushing I'm cumming again.(With her body quivering in Jack's arms, Mary starts breathing hard and lifts her legs straight up in the air and wraps them around Jack's neck.) Keep pushing deep and slow. (Mary is breathing hard. Mary demands Jack push hard loudly as she enters orgasm again.) AHHH! AHHH! I'm starting to cum again. Push harder, push harder Jack. AHHH AHHH don't stop Jack. (Holding Jack close and tight.) Honey, I'm going to cum again. Push it hard and faster, harder Jack harder. (Both holding each other tight.) I love you so much Jack. You're always so big and hard.

Jack: (Whispering to Mary.) You make me that way. I love you so much. (Jack buries his erection deep in Mary's tunnel and explodes deep inside.)

Mary: (While holding Jack tight, Mary whispers in his ear.) Got you that time. That thing is finally dwindling. I finally feel like I satisfied you. Let's wash each other down and toast our anniversary and first night alone together.

Jack: I'm all for that one. (The two sip their champagne, kiss softly and go to the shower.) Set the water the way you want it. (As he soaps Mary's body, she holds and softly kisses Jack.) You are so soft and beautiful. You have been so good to me over the years, please never stop loving me.

Mary: (The two engage in another soft kiss.) Touch me Jack. (Mary begins to pull on Jack's penis.) All it takes is a touch and you're ready. (Holding each other tightly.) Keep touching me Jack, I'm cumming, I'm cumming.

Jack: Keep pulling honey, it feels so good.

Mary: (Whispering in Jack's ear.) I love you, tell me when you're ready to cum, I don't want it in my mouth.

Jack: (Taking Jack deep down her throat, Mary slowly drives Jack nuts by slowly bobbing her head and pulling on his shaft. After awhile Jack tells Mary.) Honey, I'm going to cum. (As Mary pulls her head away and continues to stroke with her hand, Jack explodes all over the shower wall and both laugh hard.) I guess I have to clean the mess. Some running water will fix everything up.

Mary: Let's cook some shrimp, eat and swim.

Jack: I'm a little beat, let's lie around, sip champagne and eat later.

Mary: Because this a no rush evening, that is a great idea. (While looking at the depth of the water in front of him, Mary moves behind him with a playful thought and shoves Jack overboard.) Get into that water.

Jack: (When he surfaces.) Why you witch, get in here. (As Jack reaches for Mary's leg, she dives over his head and into the lake.)

Mary: Wow, the water is nice. This will be one of the times we'll tell our grandchildren about. Tell me, do you think Bill will be a smartass, shoot the flare gun off and deliver the kids to us?

Jack: I think Bill will shoot the flare gun off and make a joke about it tomorrow. Let's enjoy our evening. Let's put the mosquito net up and then make dinner. We can't forget to burn the citronella candles.

Laura: (After a full day on the water.) Honey, I want you to meet Nadine. She is Carlos Castillo's wife.

Bill: Nice to meet you. Your husband is quite a guy. Will he be here today?

Nadine: He may show up in an hour or so.

Bill: It's very nice to meet you. Your children are nice and well mannered.

Nadine: How did the two of you meet?

Bill: Many Middletown Police visit Dr. Carrie and me.

Nadine: Are you a partner?

Bill: No, I currently work the practice for him. Unfortunately, he is passing away. I am trying to buy the practice from him.

Nadine: That is unfortunate, I hope he is comfortable.

Bill: I know he is comfortable and his time will come soon. Let's talk about something more pleasant. Your children looked good on the skis and rafts.

Nadine: You have a lovely family too.

Bill: Well Carlos is arriving. Honey, let's start the grill; we have a lot of hungry people.

Laura: Sounds good to me.

Bill: (After eating, Bill tells everybody what went back and forth between the Bordowskis and him.) Carlos, Nadine and Laura, would you like to play a little game on the lovebirds? Jack and Mary said fire a flare if the kids are bad. I bet between love sessions they will be looking for a flare. Let's wait until the sun goes down and give them what they want.

Laura: (With a smile.) Tell me, what do you think the two lovebirds are up to?

Nadine: Relaxing and having a quite night under the stars.

Danielle: Oh come on, you know what they will be doing all night. Their only break will be for sleep.

Dallas: (Laughing very hard.) I'm the one you would expect to hear that one from.

Daisy: One hot night of kissing and Danielle wakes up.

Danielle: Why don't the two of you shut up?

Mary: (Back to the boat.) My goodness, a TV with a rolling stand and futons. Let's light these candles and enjoy the night on the deck.

Jack: What a beautiful night, you the stars and I all alone. What do you think the odds are that Bill and Carlos will come out to bother us?

Mary: Not very good if they know what is good for them. I think they will fire a flare or two and have a smartass comment for us tomorrow. (Mary pours two glasses of champagne and grabs Jack's hand with a loving touch. The two look into each other's eyes and softly speak.) Jack, I never bought this up, but aren't we better off out of New York?

Jack: (In a soft voice as their eyes meet.) Yes, and I couldn't have done it without you. Mary, you are my heart and soul and my reason for living. Without you none of this is possible and I would just be a cop on the beat in New York. I love you honey.

Mary: (Mary sees flares in the sky and starts to laugh.) Look in the sky; do you think the flares are from Bill?

Jack: (Laughing while speaking.) Yeah, Bill is playing one of his pranks. If Carlos came, he is in on this.

Mary: Do you think they will visit?

Jack: No, they are great friends. They know how much tonight means to us.

Mary: (Laughing really hard.) Bill is so bright but such a simpleton in some ways. Let's shut the TV off, push the futons together, and have a romantic night under the stars. (The two sit on the futons and lie back. Mary rolls on Jack and kisses him.) If you had one thing to ask me what would it be?

Jack: I don't really have any questions for you. The one thing I would ask of you is that you never stop loving these kids and me the way you do. I have had the best eighteen years of my life with you because of the way you love me. The only thing I would ask of you is to never stop loving me the way you do. (The movie ends with the two engaged in a hot kiss with a gentle breeze blowing the candle out and showing a beautiful starlit sky.)

The End
Watch for the Legacy